The Ballad of the F

Shelley Smith

For John and Rosemary Courlander
With Love

Table of Contents

Part One - "SING A SONG OF SIXPENCE"
(Nursery Ditty)

1

It was in the late summer of 1960 that the body of an unknown man was discovered in circumstances of peculiar horror by two English schoolmistresses on vacation in Haute Savoie.

The two women had been picnicking at the edge of a wood between Annecy and St Gervais-les-Bains. At the conclusion of the meal, the elder woman retired discreetly a short way into the wood. A few minutes later, the younger woman heard her friend cry out. Slightly alarmed, she jumped up and ran to look for her. She found her supporting herself against a tree, her face as pale as her blouse. She was staring at a clump of bushes, from which protruded a brown leather shoe and the end of a rumpled trouser-leg. For a moment, the two women were too paralyzed to move. And then the younger one drew a deep trembling breath and stepped forward, parting the bushes.

"Don't look," she faintly prayed her friend. "Oh, don't look!" And, turning away, was sick on the mossy path.

That the man had been murdered was gruesomely evident.

2

To trace the affair back to its germinal origin, one must start at the Unwins' party, on a certain evening in February three years earlier. For it actually all began with what Mrs Spade told Paula Buchanan, which she in turn, repeated to her husband afterwards, from whose brain was ultimately to spring the whole infinitely complex intrigue.

Massive as a crouching toad, Mrs Spade sat hunched in the Unwins' chilly back bedroom laying out the cards, her large meek white face downcast like a nun at her devotions.

Paula watched her, chin in hand, and waited for the delicious silliness to begin. Laughter and the rhythmic thumping of the radiogram rose up to them from the party below.

She was about twenty-seven at this date and more attractive now than when Rex had met her seven years ago; dark and slender, with the mobile, peculiarly expressive face of an actress, all mouth and eyes.

Mrs Spade noted her graceful attitude, noted too the unadorned neck and bare hands.

"You have an undoubted gift," Mrs Spade pronounced. "A gift you have not yet brought to fulfilment. But you will. You have great ambitions. You will attain your wish in an unexpected way... sooner than you think... I see a Heart Man, very close to you. He looks at you with love, lady dear. Can you place him? He's very close, he might be your husband," the pale protrusive eyes glanced up at her expressionlessly. Paula returned a bland noncommittal smile. "Yes," said Mrs Spade, "he's a strong character, a man who will always get his way. There's money lying over him." She moved a card with a fat puce forefinger. "I see a coffin. There's death here. You will benefit from the death of someone near to you. Great riches are coming to you, lady dear. You'll not be the one to die in want, lady, never fear."

"That sounds pretty unlikely," Paula commented dryly. "There's not a soul I know to leave me so much as a solitary silver sixpence."

"It's in the cards, lady, that's how they fall. It's all here. The cards never lie," said Mrs Spade, smiling a meek cat's smile with closed lips.

"When it comes to pass you'll remember Mrs Spade's words. She only tells you what is in the cards. Many's the lady alive this day who wishes she had listened to Mrs Spade."

"But I'm enthralled," Paula said politely. "I didn't mean to offend you."

Mrs Spade turned over a fan of cards and stared at them in a foreboding manner.

"There's tribulation here," she muttered. "I see the shadow of some dark happening. It comes upon you through a Club Man. Be on your guard with him. He brings a terrible sorrow to you. He's lying between you and the Heart Man," she said, touching the cards.

"Dear me, how very difficult," murmured Paula irrepressibly. "One knows so many dark men, it's going to be a little tricky to tell which is the dangerous one."

"That's all, dear," said Mrs Spade abruptly, gathering up the cards. "If I have given satisfaction, please tell your friends; and if all I've foretold doesn't come to pass, tell me."

*

The radiogram had got around once again to *Che sara, sara*, as Paula went downstairs, and above it, she could hear Rex booming out one of his preposterous anecdotes amid roars of laughter.

He was leaning on the chimneypiece, waving a chicken bone in one hand, while with the other he absently hugged to him some little redheaded popsie or other, rocking her gently to and fro as he talked. He was the sort of man who drew the eye as soon as one entered the room; a large tawny-bearded chap like a Viking or some splendid buccaneer of old, a gay confident extrovert of heroic stature. It would have taken a remarkably penetrating eye to see through to the hollow at the center, where dwelt the devouring worm.

For the "great good days" had vanished for Buchanan into the past. The good days for him, as for so many, had been the war years, when he served as a bomber pilot in the RAF. The days when one felt oneself a lord indeed: all the money one could use in one's pocket, plus the strange sense of intimacy with one's fellows springing from the everpresent thrill of danger; living with an intensity that was never to come again, because death was always at one's elbow.

When the war ended, he could have picked up his career once more; he was given the chance to take an engineering degree on a University grant. Instead, borrowing a "monkey" from a merchant he knew, he chose to sink it, together with his gratuity, in a one-man business: a plane for private charter.

He did well, those being the great "black market" days when there were plenty of clients with curious commissions to execute. It was the kind of lark that appealed to him, carrying as it did the breath of adventure and risk. And he saw to it that he was well paid for his trouble.

So fortunate was he in these ventures that he came to be known as "Lucky" Buchanan. But to be consistently lucky breeds its own dangers. One comes to trust too much in one's precious immunity; one becomes careless and over-confident; and no one's luck lasts for ever.

And so it happened that in September 1949, flying home solo from a Continental trip one bright morning, Buchanan's plane crashed – not far from Lydd.

He was picked up in pieces. Poor Humpty Dumpty! It took all the King's surgeons and medical men many a day to put him together again.

Lucky Buchanan! A miraculous escape, they said; he should have been killed. Fragments of the plane were found half a mile away.

Even his sanguine temperament was daunted at the prospect before him. For, by a peculiarly cruel stroke of Fate, on the morning of the accident, in a moment of quite idiotic carelessness due to haste, it had slipped his mind (for the first time in four years) to take out the customary insurance cover for the flight. So there it was. No cover: no claim. In a matter of ninety seconds, he had lost plane, capital, business. His whole future – gone. He had no idea in the world what he should do next – if he ever did get out of there on his two feet. (On that point, the authorities were chary of committing themselves. It did not do to discourage a patient. It did not do to raise his hopes uselessly either. Privately, they were of the opinion that he could never lead a normal life again. They were not sufficiently acquainted with Buchanan. His determination was surprising.)

When he eventually left the hospital – hobbling on two sticks, and a stone underweight – he hadn't even a place to go.

He propped himself on the bar of the first pub he came to, knocked up by the exertion of walking two blocks. And then he noticed this cute little skinny dark girl with a chap called Victor, who'd been in his squadron back in '43.

That was how he met Paula.

She was nearly twenty then, with long dark hair swinging round her shoulders, and a face that held Rex's fascinated gaze like running water; a face that was neither pretty nor ugly, a face that could seem beautiful at one moment and plain the next. After the neat aseptic prettiness of the hospital nurses with their cheerful practised smiles, Rex was ravished by this girl with the burning dark eyes and sulky mouth.

Victor said she was an actress.

"Of course!" Rex exclaimed heartily. "I knew I'd seen you before."

The girl's eyes sent him a brief sardonic gleam.

"You needn't bother. I've had *two* public performances – a couple of lines in a one-night show of *Blood Wedding*, and a cough-and-spit in radio. I wouldn't say I was exactly *famous*."

"Never mind, ducky. One of these days you're going to knock their eyes out," Victor assured her, clapping an arm about her shoulders.

"She's knocked mine out already," said Rex, smiling down at her.

But she wasn't looking at him, her long black hair falling over her cheek, she gazed down at her grubby fingernails and muttered: "One of these days, if they'll only give me a *chance*…"

All the same, it was she who suggested that Victor put Rex up for a few days, just while he looked around.

It was she who, listening like Desdemona bemused to Rex's extravagant tales, first put it into his head to write them down.

"Good grief, darling, I'm not one of those long-haired boys. I wouldn't know how to begin!"

"You could if you tried. Anyone can."

And since he too believed that he could do anything he set his mind to, and since there seemed no job available for a person still so crippled, and since he had endless time on his hands, he did pick up a pencil one idle foggy afternoon and began to scribble down a story as it came to him.

It was as simple as that. All you had to do, he found, was to go on bashing it down until you came to the end, and you had a book. And when it was done, you had it typed. And then you went to the Public Library and looked up the list of publishers and picked out one at random

13

because you liked the name (and if they didn't like it, there were plenty of others).

But Rex, as usual, was lucky and he hit on the right publisher first time. On the strength of his "advance", he and Paula rushed out and got married. A crazy penniless couple, crazily in love (but at any moment, Paula might be offered a part in some play that would run for months, and anyway Rex could always write another book).

And that was how Rex became a professional writer. Not for any love of the craft – he had no interest in the work for its own sake – it simply happened to be the immediate occupation that turned up for him, and as he used to jest: "It's nice clean work, and you can do it at home."

They were fortunate enough to find a self-contained flat at a reasonable rent in one of those old Bayswater houses off Leinster Gardens: a small dark entry leading through an archway to two largish high-ceilinged rooms, kitchenette, and bath.

There was no place in it where Rex could write in solitude. For that occupation, he rented a basement-room in Notting Hill, a small dank chamber looking out on an unedifying area with a coal shed and dustbins. And in this wretched place, he sat daily, on a kitchen chair, at a table picked up for five shillings in the Portobello Road, trying to earn a livelihood for the two of them by nothing more substantial than his wits.

Industriously, he banged out half a dozen books a year. Measured only in terms of the labor involved, it is quite something. To spin six different plots a year – even to a formula; to invent a fresh set of characters for each – however rudimentarily they are conceived; and to get down some five hundred thousand words a year – however crudely – is no mean effort. And contrary to his expectations, Rex was to learn the bitter truth that writing does not become progressively easier with practice, it becomes harder. He discovered that the mere act of writing depletes one's spontaneity, the flow of invention gradually dries up.

Writing is the only trade where you learn as you go (you could say a writer's apprenticeship lasts his whole life long). As Rex regained his strength he would gladly have found some other job, but he had no training, and without a penny piece behind him he could not hope to begin anew, thirty-five years of age was too old. He was caught in the trap. And the trap, in his philosophy, was strictly for fools. A man, he believed, should be able to master circumstances and direct his life in the way he meant it to go. It should be a simple matter, if one knew what one wanted; it was only a question of energy and will: so he believed. To discover that he had not the force of character to organize events into a pattern determined by himself came as a brutal shock to his self-esteem. For a man to have to admit to himself that he is a failure can be disastrous. And Buchanan had come to that point where his sense of futility was goading him to take some savage revenge on life.

Paula was too young to believe in the finality of failure: she still dreamed of triumph and applause. But as time passed she began to recognize a kind of desperation in Rex's embrace to which something in herself responded.

In 1957, at the time of the Unwins' party, he was thirty-eight, and Paula did her best to keep him amused. He was still as passionately in love with her as in the first days of their marriage.

Thus it came about, as they drove home through the rain in their ancient Humber on that February evening, that just for the laugh she told him of the fortune Mrs Spade had promised.

"Short of winning the Treble Chance, baby, I wouldn't count on it."

"It can't be that, darling. She said the money comes through a death."

"Maybe *Swing for the Hangman* will turn out a best seller."

"A *death*, darling."

"So what else are my books about?" He changed down as the lights turned to amber, thinking bitterly, not for the first time, of the criminal waste it was that so much ingenuity and fertile invention should be put to no better use than the grinding out of an endless stream of fatuous thrillers. With his brain and wits, there ought to be some way of making real money, the sort of money this idiotic fortune teller was talking about...

There it was, and it lodged in his brain like an irritant grain of sand in an oyster shell, to be turned in the slow course of time into a pearl.

3

One wet evening in early March, Rex came home rather earlier than usual. Paula, glancing up from the dress pattern she was cutting out on the floor, noticed his blue eyes glittering with a kind of exalted fatigue.

"Any beer in the house?"

"May be a bottle under the sink," Paula said through the pins in her mouth. "You're looking very pleased with yourself. Book finished?"

"The book? No…" He wandered back to the living-room with the opened bottle and, pouring the liquid slowly into a glass, added: "I haven't touched the book for weeks." He held the glass for her to drink.

"Then what are we celebrating?" She wiped her mouth on her wrist.

"The brilliant new plot I've thought up. It's terrific! *Colossal*! It's even good!" he laughed.

"Oh great! Am I to be told about it?"

"Sure," he said. "Sure. Don't I always want your opinion?" But he seemed in no hurry to begin. He went over to the darkened window and stared out into the street abstractedly. Lamplight glistened on the wet pavements. A woman went by, her scarlet umbrella shot with mauve in the blue evening light. He drew the long curtains across to shut out the dismal night.

"It's about a chap who plans a series of insurance frauds," he said slowly, pacing restlessly along the edge of the carpet. "He begins by insuring his life for, say ten thousand, and in course of time – I'm not going to bother you with details now, I just want you to get the feel of it – anyway, he pretends to fall ill. And apparently he dies. Apparently the body is cremated. See? All in order. Our chap then disappears. Takes on a new identity, and waits for his wife to join him when she has collected the insurance money. Simple?" He stretched himself out on the old Victorian sofa, squinting up at the glass he was turning round and round against the light.

Paula, crawling about the floor like an elegant fly in her black jersey and tapered slacks as she recklessly slashed between the islands of tissue paper, said:

"I love it. Go on."

"Well, then, this chap reinsures himself in his new identity, and in due course the business is repeated – but this time with a different *modus operandi…*"

Paula sank back on her heels and let the scissors drop from her hand as she listened.

"It's fabulous," she said with a little laugh, when he had at last completed the tale in all its elaborate detail.

"You really like it?"

"It's terrific, honestly. A real winner."

"I think so. It can't fail." He added pensively: "But I don't intend to write it."

"*Rex*! Are you crazy? Why ever not?"

"It's too good to waste."

"How do you mean, waste?"

"Look, darling, if I make it into a book all I can hope to get for it is a few hundreds. I can put it to better use. It isn't often that one has an idea worth a fortune."

She knelt upright, staring at him in perplexity.

"I don't understand."

"Don't you? Come here, baby, and I'll explain. I can't talk to you when you're so far away."

She stepped across the littered floor and perched at his side on the narrow couch. His thumb stroked the smooth contour of her wrist.

"I thought you'd see it at once. That it *could happen*. In real life. You and I, Poll, are going to make our fortune; we're going to *make it happen*."

She leaned sideways to stare at him.

"You're not serious?"

"What makes you think so?"

She gave a nervous laugh:

"You must be out of your mind, darling."

"Why? It's a perfectly sound proposition. Isn't there a quotation: 'To die is gain'? I'm going to die for gain. It's as simple as that."

"Apart from a little trifling matter of criminal fraud," Paula observed tartly.

"Oh, shoo!" He laughed. "If we're going to talk about principles, how do you think the insurance companies amassed all their millions, except by defrauding people themselves. Look at the premiums I had to pay out day after day, year after year, in flight insurance, with nothing to show for it; but they didn't take that into account on the one occasion when I forgot."

Paula unwound his arm and stood up.

"In any case," she said, stooping to pick up the pieces of silk still scattered about the carpet, "you'd never get away with it."

"Why not?"

"It's too crazy. It's absolutely crazy. Don't you *see*? I mean, it's all very well in a *book*. It may sound all right on paper, but in real life... honestly, darling, it's too utterly fantastic."

He rolled back his head and contemplated the plaster convolutions on the ceiling. "Listen, this isn't a piece of nonsense I've dreamed up on the spur of the moment, I've been working on it for weeks, perfecting every tiny detail. There's not a weak link anywhere, it's as beautiful and strong as a platinum chain. It's not only possible, it's entirely practicable."

"I'm going to make the supper," Paula said, tossing the lengths of silk into a chair.

"Not yet."

"Need we talk about it any more tonight?"

"Why, we haven't begun, baby," he said, coming behind her and grasping her elbows. Bending his head, he put his bearded lips to the soft little hollow just below her ear. "Don't you understand, it's you I'm thinking of."

"Oh, hell! You don't think I really care all that much about money, do you?" she said, but without much conviction, for it was beginning to dawn on her that this was no idle talk for a passing amusement, but an idea about which he was quite in earnest, and with a sinking at the heart she saw that the end was already predetermined.

She knew how it would be. She had been married to Rex for nearly seven years, and by now she knew the way it went. She might hold out for a week, or a month, or a year, but sooner or later, if his mind was made up, she would give in. She would give in because she loved him. Because she loved him, a part of her was afraid. Afraid that she would not be able to hold him once his passion for her died. With a shiver of apprehension, it struck her that it was through his craving for excitement and adventure that she could exploit his need for her. Perhaps all Lady Macbeth's furious ambition amounted to no more than a woman trying to keep her husband at her side, by offering him what his heart desired.

She sighed, gently disengaged herself from his embrace, and went into the kitchen. And all the while, she was preparing the meal and laying the table, Rex followed her around, telling her his plan all over again point by point.

"You've always said what a good actress you are. I'm giving you the chance to prove it," he said, appearing at the kitchen door as she washed up.

"I know."

"You'll never have a more testing role than this. It'll make every kind of demand on you."

"I believe you," Paula said, untying her apron. "Shall we go round to The George for an hour?"

But even in the pub he could not let it drop for long. He was fascinated by it, like an acrobat who has invented some incredible new way of plunging through the air, tempted by the very hazards against which he must pit all his nerve and skill and agility.

Even when they were in bed, in the very act of making love to her, he suddenly muttered: "In any case, I wouldn't do a thing till next year."

"Oh, *Rex! Please!*" she cried, pushing him away and turning her back. "No, leave me alone. I can't stand any more of it. I shall *scream* if you mention it again."

"Good lord, Poll! What's the matter?" he exclaimed in absolute amazement. "Am I boring you?"

"It's just that we've had it now for five hours non-stop: it becomes *inexpressibly* tedious," she said through her teeth, her eyeballs glaring in the dark.

"Well, why didn't you say so before, Polly? I'll shut up. There's no point in talking about it if you're not interested, is there? You know I couldn't attempt it without your connivance." For there was the root of the matter. Without Paula, he could do nothing. She was the indispensable factor in a plot so complicated that it would take three years to execute in its entirety, the one true accomplice on whom he must depend. 'The two of us, *contra mundum*,' he thought as he fell asleep.

True to his word, Rex said no more. He had set the idea in Paula's head; the mechanism could now go on ticking away on its own.

"Poor darling, he was horribly disappointed," Paula told herself next morning, as she ran the hoover over the carpet, the stray pins rattling in its insides. "I might have shown a little enthusiasm. It was rather mean of me, after all the time he'd spent working it out. Because it *was* a clever idea. Fantastic, of course, but queerly impressive. Only, it simply wouldn't have done for me to encourage him. One of us must keep our heels on the ground. He's like a little boy planning a nursery raid, he doesn't foresee the outcome, he's only thinking of the fun." And she smiled to herself, ruefully, as she scoured the breakfast dishes...

"I suppose it might be made to work," she thought in the greengrocer's, her eyes wandering from the polished apples to the golden bunches of carrots and smoky-violet cabbages...

"It'd be a tremendous lark," she decided, imagining herself playing the part, while the little needle clicked its way across the length of silk she was guiding through the machine...

And standing before the mirror, fitting on the half-made dress, she caught sight of her solemn face, which caused her to remark aloud to her reflected image: "You silly little fool, what are you thinking of! You'd be scared to death." Indeed, her heart was beating just as though some ordeal lay ahead of her.

She did her best to forget about it (though it had an unfortunate way of popping up again when she was passing a jeweler's window, or a particularly elegant woman, or a new car half a mile long and all a-dazzle with chromium; it was as if some small malicious devil was nudging her with his sharp elbow: "You too... why not?")

She was beginning to hope Rex had given up the idea, when he announced carelessly one evening, while they were waiting for their dinner-guests to arrive: "I've just paid the first premium on a Life Policy for ten thousand pounds with Standard Assurance."

She damned nearly dropped the casserole. She turned to him a white face.

"You don't really mean you're going through with it."

"I haven't spent a hundred and eighty pounds on a premium just for fun, ducky."

She locked her arms round his neck.

"Please, Rex darling, don't do it."

"What is there to be afraid of, baby?"

She gave a shaky laugh.

"I don't want to go to prison."

"You do surprise me." His hands slid into her brief cap sleeves to caress her shoulders. He leaned his cheek against her hair. "Would I let you go to prison? Would I let anything happen to you? Am I a fool? But without the spice of risk where would be the adventure? Aren't the stakes worth it? A hundred and twenty thousand pounds," he exclaimed, rolling the words around his mouth like wine. "My God, it makes me dizzy to think of it!" He laughed, hugging her close. "It's going to be *fun*, baby, the most enormous fun you can imagine," he promised.

In his arms, she could believe it. When he was holding her, it was impossible to be fearful. He was so confident and strong that it seemed absurdly niminy-piminy to be qualmish.

And of course, as time went on, she not only became inured to the idea, by dint of rehearsing it over and over with Rex, it came to seem like some private theatrical performance and all the difficulties and dangers of the outside world receded into unreality. Little by little her moral attitude underwent a complete reversal. They were bound together by a conspiracy that separated them from everybody else, and this secret gave her a sweet warm feeling of security. It made her feel that the two of them were alone together against the rest of the world.

4

Rex had no intention of beginning operations until after the second premium had been paid. (Any Insurance Company would have a perfect right to be suspicious if a healthy chap in the very vigor of life should kick the bucket just after taking out a Life Policy; it would look too damned convenient.) There were many things to be done and many curious objects to be procured before then by way of preparation: from a set of teeth in a pawnbroker's window, the purchase off the peg of a formal dark business-suit such as he did not possess, a secondhand car, and the opening of a new bank account, to a skull he had seen adding a macabre touch of fantasy to some bric-a-brac in a shop off Cecil Court.

But his first task was to obtain some Digitalis, a drug used in certain diseases of the heart, which could only be procured – legitimately procured, that is – through a doctor's prescription.

He said to Paula at breakfast:

"It's time I paid Old Joe a visit. I rather thought I'd go round there this evening. Don't wait supper for me."

Old Joe and his wife were the caretakers of the house in Craven Hill Gardens where Paula and Rex had lodged before they were married. Old Joe was an amusing old character who had been many things in his time – from a bookie's tout in Bethnal Green to Montana cow puncher, with somewhere along the line a short sweet interlude of six weeks as a millionaire. The two men swopped yarns with mutual pleasure. When Rex was feeling stale or stuck for a plot, a visit to Old Joe would often spark off an idea.

"Why, if it isn't Mr Buchanan!" cried Mrs "Joe" as she opened the door, beaming at him with her black fangs.

"And how's my favorite girl?" Rex inquired, lifting the old tub off her feet and swinging her around.

She shrieked with pleasure, like a child.

"Oh, Mr B, Mr B, put me down! Aren't you awful!"

"Thought it must be you," observed Old Joe, shuffling up behind them in the dark passage. "When Kitty lets out a cackle like that, it couldn't be no one else but Mr Buchanan. Come in, come in. Long time no see. How you been keeping?"

"Busy, busy," said Rex, unloading his pockets.

"Still writing at them books of yours?"

"That's it. Here, sweetheart, take these off me, will you? The candy's for you, the fags for Joe, and the beer for all of us."

"Oh, Mr B, you shouldn't have, you really shouldn't," the old girl protested.

"Come off it, Gorgeous! A figure like yours must take some keeping up."

"Oh, I am a size! I don't get any thinner, do I?"

"You're lovely. Ask Joe. You're just the way he likes it – as much as he can get for the money."

All the while he was joking, his quick eyes were roving about the room looking for something he could use – a rough edge, a sharp corner, a protruding nail... there appeared to be nothing suitable. It was the old woman who provided him with the opportunity.

Joe said:

"What about this beer, then. Let's have some glasses, old girl."

She reached into a cupboard and brought out a couple of glasses.

"Hey, what's this? Aren't you having any?"

"Gives her the wind, Mr B."

"Well, have a lollipop, have *something*," said Rex, seizing the box, and, taking out his penknife, he slit it sharply across its sealed edge with a movement so violent and clumsy that the blade skidded from the corner of the box into the fleshy cushion at the base of his thumb.

He swore, and dropped the box.

"Oh, Mr B, what have you gone and done?" the old woman cried.

"It's nothing," he said, looking at the blood.

"Oh, it's nasty, isn't it. Let me get you a bit of plaster."

"Not to worry, old dear. I'll run the tap on it, that'll stop it bleeding."

"Oh, yes, do. Give it a good wash, Mr B, that knife of yours might be skeptic."

"Bathroom's on the left," foe called after him.

Must have been the first one ever built, he thought, as he locked the door, observing the crumbling plaster, the encrusted verdigris, the stains bright as lichen in the bath. His face in the mirror on the fretted, stained-oak medicine chest was all lopsided, one blue eye round and huge and a nose grotesquely twisted; his grin wavered back at him with tombstone teeth and a harelip. "That was very nicely done, old sport," he said to his reflection, turning on the tap and letting the water run over the cut.

He searched among the tins of salve and packets of cornplaster, the laxatives, the bandages, the denture-sticking powder, the camphorated oil and Langdale's Essence of Cinnamon, till he came across a small bottle labeled 'Digitalis'.

The contents he carefully transferred, drip by drip, into an empty two-ounce bottle he had brought with him, rammed the cork home, and put it back in his pocket. The empty Digitalis bottle he smashed against the tap and swept the glass fragments into the basin, so that it should appear to have been dropped there accidentally and its contents spilled down the waste.

He unlocked the door and came out, a handkerchief wound round his hand, and a concerned expression on his face.

"Joe, I've done something frightful. I've had an accident with that heart-stuff of yours. I was poking about in the medicine-chest for a spot of disinfectant, and I knocked the bloody bottle into the basin and broke it to smithereens."

"It doesn't matter, Mr B."

"I'm dreadfully sorry."

"Think nothing of it. Plenty more where that come from. Kit'll doddle round to the surgery and explain to the doc. Won't you, old girl? Nothing she likes more than a nice sit in the waiting-room for an hour or two. The tales she comes back with, you'd never credit," he said with a guffaw.

Rex said scrupulously:

"You must let me pay for it, that's the least I can do to make amends," and he laid a shilling on the plush table-cover.

5

If Bertram Henderson had not already been the Buchanans' physician, he was just the doctor Rex would have chosen for his purpose. He fitted the bill admirably, for two reasons. One, that he had a wife and two school-age sons, whom they usually took abroad for the summer holidays; and the other, because Henderson ran his practice without a partner.

Dr Henderson was a bluff sandy-haired chap, who encouraged his patients not to think too much about their ailments. The Buchanans were healthy enough not to require his services very often; his relations with them were more social than medical. For since both the Buchanans and the Hendersons had large circles of friends and lived in the same district the circles were bound to overlap.

Towards the end of the year, Rex went to see him professionally, having taken a dose of Old Joe's medicine just beforehand. Even though he knew what to expect, he was surprised at the effect it had on his heart; the sensation was quite disagreeable.

He said casually:

"Bertram, I wish you'd be a good fellow and just run your thingummy over me."

"Hallo, what's the trouble?"

"Nothing, I hope. Only I keep getting a damned funny pain around the old wishbone. Dare say it's nothing but indigestion."

"Well, strip off and we'll see. I expect you don't take enough exercise."

"My dear old medico, it's precisely when I do take exercise that the pain comes on."

"How long have you had it?"

"Couple of months, I should say."

Henderson finished auscultating and straightened up.

"I think we'll take an electrocardiogram."

"Then it is my heart," Rex said quickly.

"My dear chap, there's no need for alarm. You can't expect to be as fit as you were twenty years ago. It doesn't mean you're going to die, you know. There's no reason why you shouldn't live to a ripe old age."

"I hope so. All the same, I'd rather Paula didn't know about it. I don't want her worrying. So we'll have a little of this famous professional secrecy you doctors are supposed to go in for, if you don't mind."

*

The following April he duly paid down the second premium on his policy with Standard Assurance. A month later, he had finished the last book on his contract and took it along to the publisher.

Talbot, the publisher, was a willowy gentleman with a dark little Vandyke and glasses, who collected cinquecento drawings. He offered a limp moist hand.

They talked a little about the new book, and then Buchanan suddenly rose to his feet and said abruptly:

"Talbot, I want to ask a great favor. There's no one else to whom I can turn. I'm in such a desperate fix, I'm half out of my mind. I need five hundred pounds, now, at once."

"My dear fellow," Talbot cut in hastily, "if it was—"

"For God's sake don't refuse me," Buchanan said in a low voice. "Paula – my wife – has to have an immediate operation. It's very serious."

At that moment, the inter-com on Talbot's desk buzzed. And while Talbot dealt with it, Buchanan turned away and struck his knuckles hard against the bridge of his nose. The pain brought tears to his eyes.

"I'm sorry," Talbot began. Buchanan was blowing his nose. Talbot could see he had been crying, his eyes were still wet. It was dreadfully pathetic to see the big bearded man in tears. Publishers are notoriously not soft-hearted persons (they can't afford to be, with authors preying on their good nature daily), but Talbot found himself strangely touched. Buchanan had "touched" him literally.

"Let me know how she gets on, my dear fellow," he murmured, as he made out the cheque.

And Buchanan assured him he would, wringing his hand with such gratitude that Talbot winced.

He drove straight to his bank, paid in the cheque and drew the money out. And that evening, Paula applied a dark color-rinse to his hair and beard. When night fell and it was dark enough for him to leave the house unobserved by the neighbors, he went off with a small suitcase and caught the night train to Manchester.

He registered at the hotel as a Mr Robert Jerome of London, and the next morning, opened a bank account in that name with Talbot's five hundred pounds.

His next move as Mr Jerome was to take out a Life Policy for ten thousand pounds with Orion Insurance Ltd. And as soon as that had gone through satisfactorily, he returned to London and became himself again.

The foundation of his new identity had been laid. The second step of the plan was accomplished. There was now nothing more to do until they learned where and when the Hendersons were going for their holiday.

*

One brilliantly hot morning in mid-July, the pavements flowering with girls in their summer frocks and the sun flashing heliographs off the traffic's chromium-trim, Paula ran into Madge Henderson in the High Street almost by chance.

"Madge, my dear, what an age since I've seen you. I was beginning to think you must be away."

"Not I, alas. Only Bertram."

"Oh, no!" Paula exclaimed involuntarily, gooseflesh pricking her bare arms. "You don't mean to tell me the wretch has gone without you?" she added in a false bright tone to cover up her too-evident dismay.

Madge laughed.

"I had to beg him to go by himself. If there's one kind of holiday that's my idea of hell, it's sitting on some chilly bank for hours on end watching Bertram fish."

"You'll be going away later, I suppose?"

"Yes. Only another fortnight, thank heaven. I can hardly wait for it. Three heavenly weeks with nothing to do but lie on the sands and *bask*!"

"Where are you going?"

"A little place called Palamos."

"Where's that?"

"Spain. Not far from Barcelona."

"What bliss! Lucky you. Will Bertram go too?"

"He's having his holiday now."

Paula caught her breath.

"We must ask him over while he's on his own and try to cheer him up."

"Yes, do, Paula. I must fly, I shall be late for my hair appointment." She stepped off the curb into the streaming traffic.

Paula caught up with her on the other side.

"Madge! When do you leave? We're giving a little party at the end of the month and we want you both to come," she improvised hurriedly.

"My dear, we leave on the twenty-eighth and it's going to be one mad rush to get the children ready in time, they don't break up till the twenty-fifth."

"Are you taking the children? I thought it was very noble of Bertram to let you go alone."

"Just a cheap nursemaid, my dear."

They laughed and separated.

Palamos, Spain, for three weeks, leaving on the 28th, Paula repeated to herself as she flew off to tell Rex. It had been a devastating moment when she discovered that Bertram was already having his holiday. But since Madge was taking the children abroad with her, it might still be possible to wangle. Rex would find a way. He was so clever.

*

A couple of days later, Rex said:

"We can do it. I see how it can be done. It'll mean playing a rather cruel trick on poor old Bertram, but it won't do him any harm."

"What sort of trick?"

"He must be decoyed away."

"How will you manage that?"

"The usual way: he'll get a telegram urgently demanding his presence over there with his family. Just to keep him from the scene of the crime."

"Suppose he doesn't go?"

"He'll go, darling. Of course he'll go if he thinks that Madge… no, not Madge. What's the name of the little boy?"

"You mean Micky?"

"Micky. That's it. He'll go if he believes Micky needs him."

Paula made a small private face and stubbed out her cigarette without comment.

"Darling, it's only a jape," Rex explained kindly. "We're working up a little mystery for him that'll tease him for the rest of his life. He ought to be grateful to us for bringing some glamor and tension into his poor drab world where everything that happens happens to other people."

Paula turned her head slowly towards him, the expression in her long dark eyes shifting in the firelight from resignation to amusement.

"You're wicked and ruthless and utterly without moral sense and I adore you," she said, shaking her head in despair.

"'Ditto, Brother Smut'," he said, linking his fingers through hers. "There's not much time left, you know; it's the eighteenth already." He counted, tapping his fingers on his knee. "The seventh is exactly half way through Madge's holiday. We'd better decide on the seventh. I'll have to make sure there's a place for Bertram on the plane that night. It's not always possible to get a passage at the last moment in August."

"And we mustn't forget the party. I told Madge there was going to be a party. We'll have to invite a few people, just in case Madge should mention it to Bertram."

"Ask as many people as you like," he said generously. "It won't cost any more."

"Only the phone calls putting them off. I'll make it the thirtieth: Madge will have left, and you'll have been ill long enough for the cancelation not to seem unreasonable."

There was a regular night-flight to Barcelona leaving London Airport at 3 am. Buchanan bought a ticket for the 8th of August at the British European Airways office.

*

The next few days were spent hunting for a suitable secondhand car. It took him three days to find what he wanted. He decided finally on a Morris Minor, taxed up to the end of the year, with a new engine scarcely more than run in.

"The trouble is," he said, meditatively prodding the back offside tyre with the toe of his shoe, "that I'm going abroad for a couple of weeks. I wonder if you could keep it for me till I get back?"

The young man smiled politely.

"I'm afraid we couldn't do that, sir. At this price it'll be snapped up right away. It only came into our hands this morning."

"You're not with me, my dear chappie. What I mean is, could you mind it for me? I'll pay for it now – spot-cash – and collect it on my return," Rex said, drawing out his wallet.

"I dare say that would be all right, sir," the man agreed hastily.

"My name is Jerome – Robert Jerome. See to the registration for me, will you?"

*

Rex was not an unreasonably heavy smoker as a rule, but since the day Paula told him of Madge Henderson's coming departure his usual consumption had suddenly shot up to over eighty a day. He took a thousand home with him that evening, which was the 23rd of July.

Isa French, a photographer's model, had dropped in for a drink on her way home from the studio. She was sitting on the floor by the hearth with her shoes off and a glass of sherry beside her.

"Hullo, darling," she said, smiling up at him dreamily, shaking back her thick blonde hair.

"Hullo, Isa," he answered vaguely, and put the back of his hand to his brow. "Paula, I've got a cracking head." She looked across at him. There was a charged silence. It lasted only a moment and then Paula said:

"Why not take some Veganin?"

"I think I will. I feel like hell." He crouched down, stretching out his hand to the fire. "Cold water down my spine." He shivered. He gave Isa a heavy-eyed smile. "What's with you these days, my beauty?"

"Fed up with men and work and life in London."

"She's off to Rome, the lucky pig."

"New job?" Rex asked with an apparent effort.

"Same old dog, it's just another bit of string." Isa set down her empty glass and lapsed into unself-conscious silence. She looked very lovely with her eyes cast down and her hands loosely folded in her lap.

"It's Eric," Paula mouthed to Rex by way of explanation.

"Oh, let's not talk about him any more, the swine," Isa said loftily. "So boring for Rex."

"What's he done now?" Rex asked. He listened to her rambling story, broken with indignant expostulations, and as he listened he rolled the cool surface of a glass against his forehead. Paula watched him. And when Isa's tale was ended, Paula said quietly:

"I should turn in if I were you, Rex."

"Do you know, I think I will, if no one minds."

6

The next morning, Paula rang Dr Henderson, only to learn that he would not be back till the following day.

"Would you like a word with Dr Henderson's locum, Dr Mackenzie?" the secretary asked.

Paula hesitated.

"Perhaps I should…" To Dr Mackenzie, she explained that her husband was rather under the weather, if he'd be good enough to call round and have a look at him.

"I'll do that," said the strongly Scottish voice.

"Could you give me some idea of the time we may expect you? I have to go out, and I don't want my husband to get out of bed to answer the door."

"I'll be there directly morning surgery's over: about ten-thirty."

That didn't give them much time to get everything ready. The bed was made up, the electric blanket switched on beneath the bottom sheet, and extra covers piled on top, while Rex lay chain-smoking in a bath as hot as he could bear. Paula brought him in a pot of strong black coffee.

"How are you feeling?"

"Terrible," he said cheerfully.

A week of chain-smoking, besides playing the dickens with his heart, had given him a vile cough.

At twenty past ten, Rex got out of the bath and dried himself. In case the doctor went into the bathroom to wash his hands, Rex squirted an air-freshener liberally about the room to kill the smell of smoke. He rinsed his mouth with a strong disinfectant, and soaked his eyes in an eye-bath filled with a stinging solution of salt and water. Suffused, watery, inflamed, they stared back at him from the mirror with the glazed look of fever.

Paula filled a small plastic sachet, about as big as a penny, with very hot water and sealed up the edge again. As the doorbell rang, Rex tucked it into his cheek. It was too flat to be perceptible there.

"This is Dr Mackenzie, darling," Paula said brightly, as she ushered the saturnine young Scot into the room.

"And how are we feeling? Not too good?"

"Shivery," Rex complained.

Mackenzie seated himself on the edge of the bed and took Buchanan's wrist in his cold fingers.

"What have you been doing to yourself?"

A quite normal, if rather silly, remark. But Paula felt the hair rising on the nape of her neck. A nervous impulse to laughter nearly overcame her. She did not dare to catch Rex's eye.

Mackenzie popped a thermometer into Rex's mouth and began to count his respiration. Rex brought his hand out of the bedclothes and drew the thermometer from between his lips for a moment, as if it was not comfortably settled – for a moment just long enough to whisk the sachet under his tongue, and he replaced the thermometer to rest against it.

When the doctor removed it a minute later it registered 102·6.

"Let me have a look at your throat, please."

Rex sat up and began to cough, turning his face away. He put a handkerchief to his mouth, coughed the sachet into its folds, and tucked it under the pillow. He lay back and opened his jaws wide to the doctor's laryngoscope. "That's a nasty cough you have there."

"Yes, isn't it? It keeps him awake."

"Has he had it long?"

"Only a few days, isn't it, darling?"

"Do you smoke much?" he asked Rex.

"No."

"How many a day?"

"Ten to fifteen."

"Well, well, I should give it up for the time being and we'll give you something to ease that cough." He took out his pad and began to scribble down the prescriptions. "That'll soon put him right. He'll be himself in a day or two. And meanwhile…"

'I wonder what he really thinks,' Paula wondered as she listened to him, or appeared to listen, nodding her head intelligently.

*

But of course Rex was not better in a day or two. And the medicines went dose by dose down the sink. Henderson came on the 26th, sat on his bed, bragged of the fish he'd caught, changed one of the prescriptions, and said he'd look in again in a couple of days – everyone was down with this summer flu.

It was hellishly boring for Buchanan, lounging about in his dressing-gown all day with nothing to do, but he had to be ready to leap into bed at the ring of a doorbell. By now, the news had got round to their friends that he was seedy and they took to dropping in to see him at odd moments.

On the 28th, Paula telephoned round and canceled the party.

It happened next day that Henderson turned up at a time when they were not expecting him. Rex had no opportunity to fake his temperature. So naturally when Henderson took it it was normal. It was an anxious moment. (Henderson said: "If it's still down tomorrow, you can get up for an hour or two.") But the following morning, Paula told Henderson his temperature had soared up again.

"Don't you see," Rex said to her reassuringly, "it doesn't matter how erratically it behaves, it only makes the illness more puzzling. And the more puzzled Henderson is, the less surprised he'll be at the result. I shall allow my temperature to become normal at least once more before I grow worse."

As he entered the second week of his phony illness, Rex started dosing himself with the Digitalis.

"It feels as if they're playing a game of ping-pong with it," he said in a breathless voice, as Henderson listened to his heart.

"What a neurotic old woman you're turning into," Henderson chaffed amiably.

"The trouble with you is you don't know what's the matter with me. You're just an ignorant quack," Rex jested back weakly. The effort made him catch his breath and he began to cough. Paula raised him up, supporting him in her arms.

"Take it easy now," said Henderson, "take it easy."

A scoffing attitude was Henderson's habitual bedside manner. It did not mean that he suspected for an instant that Buchanan's malady was anything but perfectly genuine. Like every doctor who has served in the Forces, Henderson had experience in plenty of malingering; just as in private practice he came across countless cases of psychosomatic illness produced by an inability to face some difficult situation. It never entered his mind to consider Buchanan in either role. Buchanan was happily married. Buchanan had no neuroses. On the contrary, he was essentially the type of person to exult in obstacles. One simply could not imagine him retreating into illness as an escape from something too frightening to meet; one had only to spend an hour in his company to know that nothing could frighten Rex.

*

The next tactical move was to make Henderson think it advisable for Rex to have a nurse. On the following morning when Henderson had concluded his examination, Paula closed the bedroom door and pointed to the living-room.

"Bertram, tell me the truth," she said in a low voice. "How is he really?"

He gave her a long considering penetrating stare before he replied:

"Frankly, I'm not entirely satisfied, Paula. Now there's no need to get alarmed. It's just that there are certain factors in this illness of his that I admit I do not understand. Frankly, Paula, I'd like to have a second opinion."

She looked up with a frightened face. (This was not at all what she wanted to hear. To bring in another doctor could ruin everything.)

"What's the matter?" he said.

She ran her tongue across her lips.

"Do you think he's seriously ill?"

"My dear girl," he protested with excusable irritation. Laymen were always so ready to jump to false conclusions. You had only to mention a second opinion and they seemed to think you were calling in the undertaker.

"You scare me," she said, and a tear ran down the side of her nose. "I'm so afraid, Bertram."

"What are you afraid of?" he said, patting her shoulder.

"I don't know." With her hand to her mouth, she whispered: "Afraid he's going to die."

"Of course he's not going to die. Why on earth should you imagine anything so silly?" he assured her bluffly.

"Why doesn't he get better?"

"That is precisely why I want another opinion, my dear."

"I'm sorry," she said. "Can you lend me a hanky?" But as fast as she wiped her eyes, they filled again. She had the wonderful faculty – God's gift to an actress, or indeed to any woman – of being able to command tears at will; she had only to turn away her face a moment and think of something sad, for the tears to well up. "I'm sorry," she repeated. "I seem to be losing my grip. I wish you could give me something to buck me up. I'm so tired I can't think straight. I've had no sleep for five nights."

"We'll have to see what we can do about that. We can't afford to have you getting knocked up too." He lit a cigarette and sent out a stream of smoke. "How would it be if we got in a night-nurse for a few days? For your sake, my dear, just so that you can catch up on your sleep?"

"You are kind, Bertram. I must seem awfully feeble to you. I don't know what Rex will say about it."

"Then we won't ask him. You leave it to me."

"He hates strangers – strange women."

"Leave it to me," he repeated, going into the hall. "I'll get on to the Nurses' Co-operative right away."

"Bertram! I've had an idea. We've a friend, an Australian, who's a trained nurse. She was a Sister at Brisbane Hospital actually. She's terribly good at her job and a great dear. Would you mind if I asked her to take over?"

"Not in the least."

"I know Rex would prefer it."

"Is she available?"

"I'll have to find out. If you can wait just a moment I'll try and get her right away," Paula said, picking up the telephone and dialing a number. While she listened to the double ring, she said: "Perhaps you know her. Her name is Jenny McCarthy."

Bertram shook his head.

"She must be out," Paula said at last. "I'll try again later. I'll tell her to get in touch with you, shall I?" And as she opened the door to let him out, she added, drooping a little with weariness: "Can we leave the other matter over till tomorrow? Then we can discuss it more fully."

*

"Oooh!" she said, leaning against the bedroom door, "he gave me a bad moment. He wants to call in another doctor."

35

"But that's very good, Poll. That's excellent. It means he's getting worried. You should have agreed."

"Better to agree tomorrow. I've put him off till then. We don't know what sort of consultant he proposes to bring in. It'll be a specialist for sure. And it might not be so easy to fool some beastly diagnostician."

"Darling, you're too easily fooled yourself. You seem to think doctors have magical powers." He smiled at her and shook his head. "They haven't. They are no less gullible than other mortals, no less at the mercy of their own imaginings."

"Anyway, we've got Jenny."

"Jenny?"

"The nurse. I'll ring him about two o'clock, might just catch him at lunch." She walked up and down the room rehearsing her accent, drawling out the misshapen vowels, pitching her voice half an octave higher than her usual tone.

And Rex, listening, corrected and advised.

The clock on St Botolph's steeple down the road struck two. "Here we go," Paula muttered, picking up the telephone. But Henderson was out. "Will you tell him Nurse McCarthy rang. If he'd like to contact me he can get me at Freemande 02828," which happened to be the number of a call-box in Kensington, as Paula had verified. *If* he rang and *if* some inquisitive passer-by should answer and explain that neither Nurse McCarthy nor anyone else could live there since it was a telephone booth, it would merely appear as if Henderson's secretary had taken down the number erroneously.

During the afternoon, Benita Unwin looked in to see how Rex was progressing. Paula executed a double feint: first the loud cheerful manner assumed for the patient's benefit, describing his improvement and how she expected him to be up in a couple of days; and then, later, taking Benita into the kitchen on the pretext of making tea, she shook her head, looked grave, and admitted that Henderson was so concerned about him that he was calling in a second opinion, and had insisted on a nurse.

"Ah, darling, you mustn't upset yourself," Benita urged. "Rex is terribly strong. Wonderful vitality. And that's what counts, you know."

"That's what I keep telling myself."

It was a little after nine o'clock that night that Henderson rang the Buchanans to tell Paula that he had been trying to get hold of Nurse McCarthy but there had been no reply from the number she had given.

"She's here, Bertram. Would you like to talk to her? …Hang on." She put down the phone, walked into the bedroom, pulled a face at Rex, and went back to the telephone. "Hellow! …Daktor Henderson? This is Nurse McCaathy," said the high soft voice with its unmistakable Australian twang. "Mrs Biuchanan told me you wanted me to tike on Mr Biuchanan's kise, so I kime right awaiy. If you'd kear to give me your instructions, daktor… sure… sure… I understand… right… goodbye."

Her forehead was wet with nervous perspiration by the time she rang off.

"That was great," Rex said from the doorway.

"Was I all right, honestly? I was shaking."

"You were fine, baby."

"I'll make out my night report while I think of it."

She took one of Rex's unused notebooks and in a round careful hand wrote:

Temp, at 8.30 pm: 103.2

Pulse: 118

Resp.: 42

Below this, she mentioned the times the various medicines had been given, and what nourishment the patient had managed to take.

Slept from 11.45 to 2 am. Very restless. Periodically disturbed by coughing. C/o pain, region of heart.

Paula produced this report when Henderson paid his morning visit next day, which Nurse McCarthy (who had already gone off duty of course) had left for him to see.

"Have you thought any more about a second opinion?" he asked.

"I think it would be a good idea."

"There's a man by the name of Rogerson Hart, a Wimpole Street consultant. I may not be able to get hold of him today. I'll let you know."

"Thank you, Bertram. I do appreciate all you're doing, believe me," she said on a note of controlled emotion.

"Nonsense, my dear," he said, picking up his hat. "Cheer up! He's going to be all right, you know."

When he had gone, Rex put through a call to the garage where he had bought the Morris Minor.

"This is Mr Jerome speaking," he said, and reminded them of the transaction a fortnight earlier. "Can someone bring the car round this evening? Any time after seven. My wife will be here to receive the logbook and papers. You won't forget, will you? It must be delivered this evening."

For the last two days, the weather had been horribly close, a feeling of thunder in the air.

"I wish to heavens the storm would come, if it's coming," Paula exclaimed irritably, gazing out at a clear blue sky.

"It's ideal, my dear girl. No one could expect a dead body to keep in weather like this."

"Don't be disgusting."

"Come on. How about another game of Russian Bank?"

"No."

"You owe me twenty pounds."

"I don't care if I owe you a hundred. We've been playing for three hours and I'm sick of it. Can't you understand?"

"It's to keep your mind off it, darling."

"Rex, supposing there is a storm tonight. Have you thought, they might cancel all flights?"

"You are jittery, darling, aren't you?"

"This is worse than any First Night waiting for 'Curtain up'. I'm quaking inside."

"Do you want to call it off?" Rex asked in a perfectly non-committal tone.

"No," she said. "No, of course not. Not now."

"Sure?" he said. "There's still time to back out if you want to."

"No," she said. "It's only the waiting that gets me down. I shall be all right."

"Let's put on that voice record once more."

They had been listening to it at intervals all day. For it is much easier to imitate a voice than to invent one. And later that night, Rex would need a voice at his command as unlike his own as Nurse McCarthy's was unlike Paula's.

"Let's not," said Paula. "Please, darling, let's not listen to it again just yet."

He laughed, and pushed her gently on to the sofa.

"No, Rex not…"

"Relax, baby."

"Oh, darling…"

"Darling…"

"Love me," she implored urgently. "Love me, love me …

At a quarter to eight, there was a ring at the door. Paula opened it, fearing to see Henderson with Rogerson Hart, but it was only a young man with a large envelope.

"Mrs Jerome?" he said.

"Oh, you've brought the car," Paula said, smiling with relief.

"Sorry, am I late? I was told any time after seven."

He handed over the envelope and the keys; and she signed the receipt.

"I parked it just beyond the lamp-post. Will that do?"

"Perfectly, thank you. Goodnight," she said with a pleasant brisk nod, and closed the door.

After that there was nothing to do but wait, constrained to help the hours pass with more games of Russian Bank. Once Paula said: "Couldn't we start getting you ready?"

"Look, Poll, we'll take our fences as we come to them. To start mucking about with the timetable now might wreck the whole bloody show."

Strictly speaking, an air ticket may be canceled up to the last half hour before the scheduled Time of Departure and the money will be refunded. But at 12.30 am (on the 8th of August, that is to say), Paula went into the hall and dialed Skyport 3131, asked for "Iberian Flights" and when she got through informed them that Mr Buchanan was obliged to cancel his seat for the 3 am flight to Barcelona owing to illness.

Rex took the instrument from her. It was then 12.45.

"Here we go," he said, squeezing her hand. "Over the top!" He repeated aloud a phrase or two to test his voice. And then he lifted the receiver and dialed Dr Henderson's number…

7

Dr Henderson was comfortably asleep when the noise drilling into his ear blasted him out of unconsciousness. Alarum...? Night-bell...? Telephone...? His confused and drowsy brain tried to differentiate the sound. He fumbled round the pillow for the lamp switch, screwing his eyes tight shut against the cruel brightness, and picked up the phone.

"Bayswater 07453," he yawned, trying to remember which of his patients was near labor.

A male voice, brusque, flat, said:

"I have a telegram for Henderson."

"Yes? Henderson speaking."

"It was handed in at Palamos, Spain, on the seventh of August at sixteen-o-five hours."

At the words "Palamos, Spain" Henderson came sharply awake, cold to the roots of his hair with apprehension.

"Go on, please!"

"Message reads: 'Micky still unconscious desperately anxious please come.' Signed: 'Madge'. I will repeat it. 'Micky still unconscious. Desperately anxious. Please come. Madge.' Have you got that?"

"I've got it," he said numbly.

"Will you require a confirmatory copy?"

"It doesn't matter," he said, and his hand slowly dropped on to the covers. He sat awkwardly bunched against the pillows, staring blankly ahead, still grasping the dead receiver in his hand, his eyes roving ceaselessly to and fro, as though reading off invisible words on the wall opposite – the words that repeated themselves over and over in his brain:

Desperately anxious... Please come... Micky still unconscious... Desperately anxious... Micky still unconscious... Please come... Please come... Micky still unconscious...

An accident. That's what it was. There'd been an accident. There must have been a previous communication from Madge – a letter perhaps, which he had not received – telling him what had happened. He tried to imagine what could have happened. He tried *not* to imagine what could have happened. But the images presented themselves to his reluctant and terrified mind in sickening succession. He saw his little boy lying at the side of the road, hurled there in a cloud of white dust by a speeding car; he saw a stone flung by some child in play, crack on his son's temple; he saw him crashing through the branches of a tall pine; in imagination he gazed down from the edge of a precipice at a small crumpled figure on the wave-washed rocks below…

Madge was not one to give way to hysteria; she would never have sent for him if it had not been serious. He tried to recall what time the operator had said the telegram was handed in. He rooted it out of his brain. Sixteen-o-five hours, that was five past four. Five past four *yesterday afternoon*. Why on earth hadn't she telephoned? Surely that would have been simpler than telegrams, so dreadfully brief, and letters that went astray.

Perhaps she *had* tried to phone him and he had not been at home. Poor Madge, she must be frantic! He must get on to her at once. He sprang out of bed, whipping on his dressing-gown as he ran from the room…

*

"Now!" said Rex, looking at his watch. "You're on stage, Poll!"

She drew a deep breath…

This was the crucial moment, when Paula had to ring the doctor and tell him that Rex was dead – had just died of a heart attack, and then play out her tragic situation for all it was worth in order to get him to sign the death certificate on the spot. The critical part was in making contact with him at the exactly right moment. If they left it too long, he might have already left for the airport. Too soon was even more of a danger, for he might decide he had time to come round and examine the "corpse" for himself.

"It's engaged," she said a minute later. She gave a rueful nervous laugh. "All that for nothing," she said, letting herself flop exaggeratedly. "Old jelly-legs Paula!"

"We'll try again in five minutes."

*

Henderson rummaged in his desk for one of Madge's letters. Two he found, written on her own paper. There must somewhere be a letter on the hotel writing paper; the original letter confirming the bookings, if only he could find it. He remembered the name of die pension but he

41

could not recall the name of the proprietor. He came upon it at last: San Domingo del Mar. Proprietario, Juan Gonzales.

He picked up the telephone. *The line was dead.* Oh, God, he thought, oh, God, not now! He dialed "O" hopefully, but nothing happened, the line was as flatly unresponsive as before. And then it came into his head that he must have left the receiver off upstairs. He ran up to the bedroom and found it lying in the sheets. He replaced it, waited a moment and dialed "O" again.

"Number please."

"Continental Directory."

"What number are you?"

"Bayswater 07453. Please hurry, it's urgent."

"One moment, please."

*

"Rex, it's still engaged."

*

"I want the telephone number of the San Domingo del Mar Hotel, Palamos, Spain. It may be under the name of Juan Gonzales."

He had to spell every word, and then was left hanging on, it seemed to him, interminably. He was almost crying with impatience.

"I'm afraid there's no San Domingo del Mar in the directory. There are two Juan Gonzales listed: one is a notario, and the other is prefixed Don; but neither has San Domingo in the address."

He already knew that was how it would be. The pessimism of fear convinced him of it before the operator confirmed it. The responsibility and the guilt was his. It was by his choice, his own free choice, they had gone to this small inn on the mountain above Palamos, an inn so primitive it could scarcely boast of running water, much less a telephone – and all because it was cheap. And now he could not even let her know that he was coming.

How soon could he get to them, he wondered, looking up London Airport in the book. In an agony of distress he kept thinking: 'Micky needs me; Madge needs me: God, let me get there in time!' as he tried to find out about planes for Barcelona and was switched from one official to another. For the telegram had been sent yesterday afternoon and that meant that whatever it was that had happened must have happened at least two days before that for Madge to suppose he would already have heard about it. And the child was still unconscious. That could be concussion, a fractured skull; coma, perhaps.

The 10 am service was completely booked, he was told. The next flight was not until 6 pm. Quite casually, as it were by chance, the clerk mentioned that there was a seat available on the night service, leaving London Airport at 3 am, if that was of any use.

Henderson glanced at the clock on his desk. He could just make it, he decided. He *had* to make it.

"Keep it for me," he said. "I'll be there."

*

"What can have happened?" Paula laid the instrument back on its rest for the eighth time. "He can't be speaking to the Airport all this while. Something's gone wrong." She shivered. "What shall we do?"

"You'll have to go there."

"Where?"

"To his house, of course. You can tell him you've been trying to get hold of him since a quarter to one, but the line was always engaged, and—"

"You want me to go round and play out the whole thing to his face?" she said incredulously. "You must be *mad*."

"Why?"

"I couldn't do it, that's all. I couldn't do it."

"You can. Of course you can. And you will."

"No," she said, backing away. "Listen, I've done everything you asked me and I haven't made a fuss "

"For God's sake don't start throwing a temperament now. It's not the moment for it. Do as I tell you and don't be a little fool. Get out the car and drive round there as fast as you can."

"Let me try just once more," she begged, reaching for the telephone.

He pushed her hand away.

"There's no *time* for that now. You've got to catch him before he's left the house. Don't you realize that? The whole thing will be ruined otherwise. All our work, eighteen months of planning, wasted. Nearly a thousand pounds chucked away. Is that what you want?"

She burst into tears.

"I *can't* go through with it, Rex. Don't make me. Please don't make me."

For it is one thing to act numb desperation over the phone, with the aid of "Nurse McCarthy" by way of contrast and confirmation, and quite another to have to play it out alone and face to face with him.

"All right," he said, in an even tranquil tone. "All right, I won't... no need to go on crying, Poll. I've said it's all right."

*

Henderson opened drawers, tipping their contents recklessly on the floor, as he hunted for his passport... Mmoney! He hadn't enough on him. One could hardly expect them to take a cheque at the Airport. He used to laugh at Madge for her childish habit (her squirrel complex, he called it) of hiding money in silly places. He found two pound notes in a cracked luster teapot, twenty-five bob in an empty cocoa tin, and five pounds in the telephone box. He sweated at the previous minutes wasted on this game. He had still to pack an overnight bag, and get some clothes on. And he must check supplies in his medical case and make sure he had everything he might need.

Easy now, he told himself. Don't panic. You've got plenty of time. No traffic on the road at this time of night. Apply your mind. Go at it steadily. Method.

He was practically dressed when the bell rang. He scrabbled on a sock, thrust his foot into its shoe, knotted the laces in frantic haste, and ran to the door, expecting he hardly knew what. Certainly not the white face staring at him out of the dark.

"Paula!"

She came towards him like a sleepwalker.

"I've been trying to get on to you, but your line was engaged," she said. The light caught the glistening snail track of tears on her cheek. "I had to come," she said.

"My dear, what's the matter? You're trembling." He took her by the arm and closed the door. (She was indeed, and no faking; she was petrified).

"He's dead."

"What?" He had heard but not understood. It had flashed through his mind absurdly that she was talking about Micky, that somehow the news had reached her before him.

"Rex is dead," she repeated in the same small frightened tone. "He had a heart attack and died about an hour ago."

"*Dead?*" he echoed. He took her cold hands in his. "It's not possible."

She broke into weeping.

"Come and see, Bertram. Please come and see; perhaps there's something you can do. I've read of people being brought back after the heart has stopped beating," she said in halting phrases between her sobs.

"Paula, my dear dear girl, I can't tell you…" He clasped his forehead. "I wish to God there was something I could do. Believe me, my dear, if I could I would. But the fact is—"

"Please don't let's waste time talking," she implored, the tears running down her cheeks. (She didn't need to think of anything sad now in order to cry: she cried with nerves).

"No, I mustn't waste time talking," he said quickly. "I have to leave in ten minutes for London Airport and I haven't finished packing. I've barely an hour to catch the plane for Barcelona. Micky is dangerously ill and I've been sent for."

"You mean… you aren't coming?"

"Try and understand, Paula dear, that I can't help myself. I'm sorry if it sounds harsh, but the needs of the living must come before the dead."

"But what am I to do? What am I to do?"

"The nurse is there, isn't she? She'll see to everything that's necessary." He glanced furtively at his watch. "Now be a good girl and go home. I'll come and see you as soon as I get back."

She went on standing there, as if she wasn't listening, her eyes fixed on his face.

"When you get *back*. When will that be?"

"I can't tell, of course. It depends on how I find Micky." He licked his lips, longing to be gone.

"It may be days! What about Rex? What's to become of him while you're gone?"

"Paula, I haven't time to discuss it now. I'm sorry." If she wouldn't go, he must.

She ran after him up the stairs.

"Bertram! You can't really mean to leave him till you get back, alone in the flat with me," she cried desperately.

He was trying to think of a way to rig up some makeshift apparatus for a saline injection, if Micky should need it. He looked down over the banister.

"No, no, of course not, my dear," he said hurriedly. "You must get some other doctor to make out the death certificate. Try Dr Simonson, you'll find him in the book."

She followed him into the bedroom with its frantic confusion of garments and spilled-open drawers. She had become deathly pale. (This was the moment).

"That would mean an autopsy, wouldn't it? I couldn't let that happen to Rex, I couldn't. It would be like... it's a kind of sacrilege," she stammered. "Surely you can understand how one feels about someone one loves. I couldn't bear it. Bertram, I know you're in a hurry, but I beg you, before you go, to let me have a death certificate." She looked at him beseechingly.

"My dear, I can't do that." He was shocked.

"Why can't you?"

He stuffed a clean shirt into his bag.

"Because I cannot make out a certificate without certifying the cause of death."

"He died of heart failure. He had a heart attack brought on by a fit of coughing. I was there, Bertram, I saw it." She knotted her hands together so tightly that their fingers turned white. "You know it was his heart. What else could it be? Ask the nurse."

"There isn't time," he said, running into the bathroom to collect his shaving tackle.

"I'll get on for you if you'll speak," she said, taking up the receiver from the bedside table and dialing. It gave the engaged signal – as she expected. Henderson threw his razor into the bag and zipped it shut. She dialed again, one figure only.

"Paula, I must go."

She said into the phone:

"Operator, I'm trying to get through to Bayswater 11650 and the number appears to be engaged. It's terribly urgent. Could you please tell me whether they're talking or if the line is out of order..."

Henderson banged a drawer shut.

"I can't wait any longer, Paula. I must go."

She put a hand over her ear.

"*Oh!*" she cried despairingly and dropped the instrument on to its rest. "What am I to do! He says the receiver has been left of? The hook. I can't have replaced it properly in my hurry."

"For God's sake come along, Paula. Have a little pity for me," he said through clenched teeth.

She turned her face aside and held her breath, feeling the tears collect in her throat.

"Help me, Bertram! Help me! I'm so alone."

He grabbed the bag and dashed from the room. She could hear him running downstairs. She went after him, switching off the light. She was shaking, her heart beating furiously under the threat of defeat.

He was in the consulting-room, checking the contents of his medical bag. She came in and shut the door, leaning against it with outspread arms.

"Bertram, I know your one thought is to get to poor little Micky, but it won't take you a moment to do this for Rex. It's for *Rex* I'm asking it, don't you understand? I'm not asking anything impossible or wrong. I'm only asking you to do what is, after all, your duty. Surely that's not unreasonable, is it? It isn't as though he won't be examined by the other doctor."

He snapped the catches on his case.

"What other doctor?"

"I thought there always has to be two doctors to sign the certificate for a cremation."

"You never told me he was to be cremated."

"I thought you knew: it was always his wish." She came close, exerting all the power of her feminine helplessness on the romantic side of his nature through the appealing glance of her beautiful eyes.

He thought: if Simonson sees the body... he thought: what else can I do in the circumstances...? He thought: it's five past two; I've *got* to catch that plane... he thought: how can one reason with a woman in a state of shock? I shall have to give it to her, there's nothing else for it...

"What was your husband's full name?" he said gruffly, taking a printed form from his desk drawer...

As soon as it was completed he was off, his foot down hard on the accelerator, shooting past the lights. "Poor old Rex, who'd have thought he'd go like that! Dreadful for Paula. No wonder she was distraught, poor dear. I'm afraid I wasn't very kind, but I was so agitated, scared to death I wouldn't get away in time. Otherwise I'd never have done it. I suppose I shouldn't have done it anyway. If it comes out that I've made a blunder I'll just have to stand the racket. It was for Micky's sake, not Paula's. For Micky... Micky... Micky... Drive faster, can't you? Faster! Hold on, Micky, hold on! Daddy's coming..."

He caught it, a bare minute before they wheeled away the steps.

The plane rose, the lights flowed away beneath them as it banked and turned into the darkness ahead...

8

Now they were committed. There could be no turning back; this was the point of no return, Paula realized.

"Poor old Bertram," she said uneasily, draining her second whisky as she watched Rex shaving off his beard. "It was a rotten trick. You don't know how caddish it makes me feel."

"'*And my heart is like nothing so much as a bowl,*
Brimming over with quivering curds,'"
Rex quoted.

"If you'd seen him as I did…"

"What's the kick, baby? Micky isn't hurt."

"But Bertram *thinks* he is."

"In a few hours he'll know the kid's all right. So where's the harm? It's an experience for him. I can't see that he's got anything to grumble at. He ought in fact to be bloody grateful. We've given him the chance of an unexpected trip to see his family, with a nice little mystery thrown in gratis at the end of it," Rex said, feeling his bare chin.

"Just so long as it remains a mystery. He may unravel it."

"He won't, don't worry."

"You're always so goddamned sure about everything."

"Use a little logic, dear heart," he said, seating himself on the dirty linen box and turning up his face for Paula to pluck his eyebrows into a different shape. "There's no lead. Nothing to connect the business with us in any way. Ouch! He accepted the idea that I was dead without boggling or he never would have given you the certificate, you may be sure of that. Now, just suppose for the sake of argument, that later some wild intuition should lead him on to what is in fact the right track. Then what? There isn't an atom of proof he could lay his hands on. And where the hell can he get without proof?"

"I'm sure you're right, so far as *later* is concerned," Paula said, leaning back to study the effect of her work. "It's now I'm thinking of. If he gets back here before the cremation and finds out from Simonson—"

"Who's he?"

"Simonson? He's the doctor Bertram told me to get."

"That is precisely why we have to push it through quickly. We've not been given much grace, but I don't think we need fear he'll arrive before Rex Buchanan has been fully and finally disposed of. He's got to get a plane. And that won't be so simple at this time of year. Or he'll come back overland. Either way he's hardly likely to get here till it's over. And when he does get back his first thought will be to find out where that telegram came from. Even when a telegram *exists* it is a damned complicated job to trace it. So imagine the task he's set himself trying to find out about a telegram that was never sent. By the time he's given up in despair of ever unraveling the tangle, Rex Buchanan will be no more than a little heap of ash at the bottom of an urn. After that, he can think what he likes and talk himself black in the face with Simonson, there'll be bloody all he can do about it."

"I hope you're right," she said, brushing over his eyebrows with black dye.

"Don't be so sour, darling. I know it was beastly for you, but it's over now. Just keep your eyes fixed on the future when we're going to live happily ever after."

"Are we?" she said, but not aloud, as she stirred a gray rinse into the jug of water. He bent his head obediently over the basin.

They were in the process of turning him into another person. It was a transformation, not a disguise. He was about to become his own non-existent elder brother, Bill Buchanan. He did not expect to be seen by anyone who knew him, but if such a situation should accidentally occur, any resemblance to his former self would be regarded as no more than a natural family likeness.

Where Rex wore his tawny hair combed loosely back from his forehead, Bill's iron-gray hair was parted at one side and smoothed flat with cream. Rex's bearded, fresh-complexioned face was now clean-shaven and colored the deep tan of one who religiously exercises in the open air in order to keep fit. Rex's brows rode upwards in a Mephisphelean slant above the wicked glint of his blue eye; Bill's dark brows followed the curve of the bony structure beneath the skin, and heavily-rimmed spectacles shadowed the eyes themselves.

When he was dressed, in the dark suit he had purchased nine months previously for this occasion, with a black tie in sign of mourning, he perfectly looked the part of a rather dull and respectable solicitor about fifty years old, practising in some provincial city like Norwich.

He regarded himself critically in the glass, made an infinitesimal adjustment to the handkerchief in his breast pocket, and turned round.

"My dear sister-in-law," he said, holding out his hands to her. "You must now leave everything to me. I shall see to it all. That is what I am here for, to take it off your shoulders."

And he did.

By nine-thirty, he had made all the arrangements for the funeral, put an announcement in the papers, ordered the flowers, and got in touch with Dr Simonson who said he would be round that afternoon. It was he who, shortly before noon, opened the door to the gentlemen from the West End emporium's funeral parlor. As he ushered them into the hall, Paula came through the archway looking like Lucia di Lammermoor in the mad scene in her long flowing wrapper, her hair loosened around her blanched face.

"What is it, Bill?" she asked in a voice made hoarse with tears.

But before he had time to block her view she saw the coffin they were bearing and she gave a terrible cry:

"*No*! *No*! They shan't take him away! They shan't…"

"Now, Paula dear," began her "brother-in-law" in a soothing tone, taking her gently by the arm.

"Bill, don't let them," she implored him with a look of desperation.

"There, there, now. Leave it to me," he crooned, patting her hand.

Yet something in his manner must have sounded a note of alarm for suddenly she tore herself from his grasp and ran back through the archway. The bedroom door slammed to. They heard the key turn in the lock…

"My God," the man she had called "Bill" exclaimed softly. He looked round at them with a blankly disconcerted face: "Do you know what my sister-in-law's done? She has locked herself in with her dead husband." He took out a handkerchief and passed it across his forehead. "Now what do we do?"

He tried talking to her; but it is hard to reason with anybody through a door. Indeed it proved useless. One could not even be sure she was listening. In the silences between his expostulations she could be heard weeping.

He went back to the waiting men.

"Short of breaking down the door – which would scarcely be seemly in the circumstances, I'm sure you agree – I really don't see what is to be done. I'm afraid it's not much use your waiting any longer, gentlemen. I shall have to make fresh arrangements. Don't worry, I shall explain matters to your manager myself. I'm only sorry for the trouble you've been put to," he added, shaking the senior by the hand and deftly leaving a folded note in his palm.

"Better leave that," he reminded them as they turned to go; "your colleagues will need it later."

The men looked at one another: the request was reasonable, if unusual; but then the situation itself was unusual. The coffin bumped gently down on end.

As soon as they were gone, Buchanan pushed it into a cupboard out of sight.

9

It was half past four before the doctor arrived. Even Buchanan was becoming edgy from the long empty hours of waiting.

"That must be him now," he exclaimed in relief as the bell rang at last.

And as he went to answer it, Paula picked up her handbag and slipped out the back way. She was hurrying across to their ancient Humber and indeed had her hand on the door when something rather dreadful happened.

A claw fell suddenly on her wrist, and old Miss Caldicott from the top floor croaked at her in the loud toneless voice of the deaf:

"Oh, my dear, I am so glad to see you! I've been so worried, my dear. I suppose that must sound absurd to you. I almost came down to inquire, except that one does not like to intrude, you know. But really, Mrs Buchanan dear, it did give me such a *turn*—"

Trapped, Mrs Buchanan looked helplessly this way and that, pining to escape, conscious of time racing her to her destination while this maddening old biddy burbled on, too deaf to hear her protests and excuses. Not actually listening herself, Paula caught:

"…standing at the window feeding my birdies, when I looked down and saw this coffin and it seemed to me they were carrying it into your apartment. So very relieved to find I was mistaken, Mrs Buchanan dear. Just tell me that your dear husband is all right too. Such a nice young man!"

It seemed cruel, heartless in the extreme, to lie to the poor old dear; but it was equally impossible to tell the truth. She said abruptly: "He's dead. He died last night. Forgive me; I can't talk about it." She pulled away her arm and scrambled into the car, racing the engine to drown the old woman's shocked ejaculations.

*

And after all, it was easier than he had dared hope. His palms were damp as he opened the door.

"Dr Simonson? I am William Buchanan the deceased's brother. Please come in."

The dark tubby little man bustled over the threshold.

"I'm sorry my sister-in-law isn't here, Doctor; but the fact is that the shock of my brother's death, coming on top of the strain of nursing proved too much for her; she simply collapsed and as it was out of the question for her to stay here on her own, Dr Henderson kindly arranged that she should go to a nursing-home for a few days."

Dr Simonson waved a plump impatient hand.

"My dear sir, pray don't bother to explain; I perfectly understand." His brisk manner dismissed such commonplace mysteries as birth and death.

"I'm afraid you don't, Doctor. But I assure you I wouldn't be bothering you with it if it weren't necessary. I'll be as brief as I can."

"Please do," muttered the little man, with a hint of irritation in his tone.

"Would you care to smoke?" Buchanan asked, holding out his cigarette-case with a grave smile. He had to allow Paula time to get to her post. "You see," he went on, blowing out a long funnel of smoke with a meditative air, "I have an absolutely unavoidable business appointment tomorrow morning. It means that I must leave for Norwich tonight whatever happens; and before I go I must see to it that the flat is properly closed up. Obviously my brother's body would have to be removed first, before I could lock the place up…wWhat was I to do? I had to do what I thought best." As he spoke he pushed open the bedroom door gently, revealing the wide untenanted bed stripped down to its bare mattress. In a hushed voice, he said: "They took him away scarcely an hour ago. I was hoping you might arrive before then, but…"

*

As long as the phone-booth was occupied, it looked natural enough to be hanging around, but eventually the girl with the blonde pony-tail ended her conversation and staggered out with a look of surprise into the fresh air, and Paula was obliged to stroll away and stare into a shop window.

She was beginning to wonder how much longer she would need to wait before she could safely conclude Simonson was not going to ring, when the thin shrill sound of the bell penetrated the noise of the street. She darted into the booth and pulled the door tightly to. She lifted the receiver:

"Freemande 02828. Nurse McCaarthy speaking."

"Aow, yes?"

"Yes, Daktor. I understand."

"It was."

"That's right. Twelve forty-five."

"He did."

"I did."

"No trouble at all, Daktor. Delighted to be of service. Is that all? …well, goodbye."

*

'Not strictly orthodox procedure,' thought Dr Simonson wryly as he replaced the instrument, 'but in the circumstances,' he decided, unscrewing his pen…

*

Buchanan's first arrangement had been for the coffin to remain in the flat until die funeral. Now, he had to advise the Undertaking Department of the West End store, that his sister-in-law – the widow – had just been rushed into a nursing-home in a state of collapse, and the flat would have to be closed up for the period of her absence. This sudden unfortunate change of plan meant that he must ask them to remove the coffin to their mortuary chapel so that the apartment could be locked up this same evening as he had a plane to catch…

*

By the time Paula got back, he was already at work on the coffin. It was an exacting business, the weight had to be correctly distributed and then wedged in position so securely that it could not shift.

"Want to say goodbye?" he suggested, holding up the skull towards Paula.

"Don't be disgusting!"

"Bring us luck, old dear," said Buchanan, kissing the lipless mouth. He jammed the set of false teeth between the jaws and laid the head carefully in place. "I hope it is a man's head, I never thought to ask," he remarked suddenly. "It looks rather small, now I come to think of it. Still, I don't suppose the blokes whose dainty task it is to pound up the remnants will notice a little thing like that. Boring job that must be. Wonder what they think about," he mused, as he screwed down the lid.

At nine-thirty, the coffin was collected and driven away in a plain van. An hour later, Buchanan quietly let himself out, climbed into the Morris

Minor – with Robert Jerome's logbook and driving licence in his pocket – and started off on the long drive to his new life…

10

Paula could not have felt more alone and frightened if her husband was really dead. She was in dread that Henderson would come round to see her before the cremation. He pursued her with his inquisition through her dreams, threatening to have the coffin opened, dragging her to the bier (in surroundings strangely reminiscent of Mr Sowerberry's coffin shop in *Oliver Twist*), and when he threw back the lid and forced her to look inside, there to her horror lay Dr Simonson with his eyes closed and his hands folded meekly on his breast... "You see," said Dr Simonson, sitting up and smiling at her from a face that turned into a grinning skull before her eyes...

She woke up screaming, drenched in perspiration.

*

She had no need to think of mighty poets in their misery dead in order to bring tears to her eyes at the funeral. The ceremony was a short affair, without even an undenominational address; only music. She sobbed uncontrollably all the way through. She could not have said why she was weeping, but she wept as though her heart would break. It was as if she had tapped some unknown source of emotion in her breast that gushed forth in showers of salt tears.

She had not imagined there would be so many people, that so many of Rex's friends would come to bid him farewell. It made her feel dreadfully deceitful. She thought she was struggling against an hysterical impulse to laugh; and she suddenly found herself crying, she did not know why.

Everybody was kind to her afterwards. They insisted that she must not be alone. She did not want to stay by herself in the empty flat, she admitted it. She thought she would go away for a time, after the more immediate business was attended to. Meanwhile, the Unwins took her back with them for a few days to help her over the first unbearable loneliness. For she was lonely. It was the first time she and Rex had been separated in all their eight years together.

"I will *never* go through all this again, *never*! Make up your mind to *that*," she wrote to him in Manchester. And she really believed she meant it, so great was the reaction after the weeks of tension. How difficult it is to realize the possibilities of change in oneself and how one's thoughts and feelings and ideas may alter.

The solicitor she instructed to wind-up her husband's affairs told her it would take probably three months to obtain Letters of Grant, and the Insurance Company could not pay out on her husband's Policy till then.

Three months is a long time to live alone when one is not used to it. And Rex had firmly vetoed any meeting between them. He said it was too risky. Husbands and wives were separated for longer than this during the war, she told herself repeatedly, but she could not accustom herself to it. She missed him terribly. 'Oh, never, never again,' she swore. 'He'll have to give up the idea.'

She gave notice to the landlord that she was terminating her tenancy at the end of the quarter, and tried somehow to fill her days and nights till then.

"You ought to get a job, darling," said her friends.

"Yes, I know. I shall have to do something."

"Any ideas?"

"I might go back to the stage."

"That would be marvelous of course. Do you think you could? I was thinking actually of Rita, and wondering if you would like me to give you an introduction—"

"Oh, darling, don't bother! Something'll turn up. I refuse to become a great old bore over this, nagging all my friends for help."

"Don't be silly, darling, and don't be proud. We want to help."

"It's sweet of you."

So bad for her to have nothing to do, they said, no wonder she mopes. And what does she imagine she is going to live on, they asked one another. Rex was to blame, of course, he'd spoilt her. And as for this notion of going back to the stage, what could be more hopeless! It wasn't as though she had ever made any kind of name for herself.

"I saw her once at the Royal Court. Only a small part, but I thought she was really rather good. It was a dreadful play."

"Oh, I'm sure she's good. Don't think I'm running her down. I adore her. It's just that she doesn't seem to realize her position, poor darling, I'm terribly sorry for her."

"I expect she'll marry again."

"That would be best," agreed the other.

*

Paula sold their old Humber for what it would fetch and with the proceeds went away for a few weeks, as she had promised. Boring solitary walks along the wind-swept promenade with its sparkling views produced in her only an appetite. But while she was there, she received a card from Birmingham bearing the one word 'Success!' in Rex's writing. Manchester had proved useless, Sheffield was a wash-out, Newcastle no good either. Now it seemed he had found what he sought in Birmingham.

She went back to Town and began making ready to move. The following week, the Standard Benefit Assurance Company wrote to say their representative would be calling on her next day at twelve noon, if that would be convenient. "Any time, my dear old Company, is convenient for me to receive ten thousand pounds," she murmured. "What do you think!"

Perhaps it was understandable that she should try to calm her nervous excitement by setting herself to clear out a cupboard full of old rubbish they had collected over the years: cracked vases, broken electric fires, saucers without cups, cups without handles. Plunging into the cobwebbed interior, she forgot the time. She was startled when the doorbell rang. She scrambled over the piles of junk, brushing her hair off her face with her dirty hands, leaving a smudge across one cheek. She could not imagine why the young man looked so taken aback when she opened the door.

She was a little surprised herself when he announced that he was from the Standard Benefit Assurance Company. For some reason, she had expected a dried-up elderly man with hair strung like harpstrings across a bald scalp, and instead, she was confronted by a brown young man about her own age.

"Do come in. I'm afraid I forgot the time," she said, pushing back her tousled locks, as she led him into the living-room. "Will you excuse me a moment? I must wash my hands, they're filthy." She held them up for him to see with that sweet confiding smile she used to charm strangers. It was a smile that seemed to say, You are my old and valued friend from whom I have no secrets and with whom I can share all the fun in the universe. He was not the first young man to have been turned dizzy by it.

He could not have been more disconcerted if Zeus himself had appeared to transfix his heart with a shaft of lightning. That was what it felt like: his pierced heart leaping furiously like a barbed fish within his ribs.

Silly ass, he admonished himself, nervously fingering the knot of his tie, you can't possibly imagine you're in love with a woman because she smiles at you. When she comes back I shall see it was just a momentary impression, a trick of the light or something.

When she entered the room at last, he was examining an old French plate decorated with a pen-drawing of curious Symbolist figures – a spilled glass, a pocket watch, a gloved hand, and a hanged man in a top-hat, with underneath the motto: *De ne se repentir de riett le commencement de la sagesse.*

"I'm sorry to have kept you waiting," Paula said, "I hadn't realized I was such a scarecrow."

The glance of her eyes, curiously liquid against the velvety freshness of her powdered skin, set his knees shaking. He had an absurd desire to touch the smooth inky hair flowing back from her brow.

"Fascinating old plate," he managed to say, putting it back.

"Do you like it?"

"Very unusual, isn't it?"

She said casually:

"You can have it if it appeals to you."

He flushed deeply.

"It's terribly kind of you, but I couldn't possibly," he stammered.

"Why not? I shall only sell it to some wicked old dealer. I have to dispose of everything when I leave here. So you might just as well have it if you want it."

"If you'll allow me to buy it…"

She shrugged with an air of large indifference.

"I don't suppose I should get more than thirty bob for it; it's not worth talking about." She laughed suddenly. "But I mustn't waste your time. You haven't come here to buy my junk. Let's get the business over, shall we?"

He opened his briefcase and took out some papers.

"If you will just sign this formal receipt, Mrs Buchanan, to say that we have paid you the full sum of ten thousand pounds."

She stared at him.

"But you haven't."

"I have the cheque here. I will hand it over to you directly I have your receipt."

"Well, what a cockeyed way of doing business. It's lucky you have an honest face," she commented as she put her name to the paper.

He glanced at the signature, blotted it, and folded it away.

"And here's our cheque for ten thousand pounds," he said, handing it to her.

She took it from him in silence, gazing down at the slip of paper between her fingers with an unfathomable expression.

"Well…" he said. He snapped the clasp of his briefcase. "Well, I think that's all." He glanced round in search of some reason to stay. "Did you really mean—" he gave an unnatural laugh, "—that I might have that plate?"

He wondered what she was thinking, her gaze was so remote and strange, lost in some private world from which he was excluded. And then she came out of her thoughts and smiled her heavenly smile.

"Certainly. Of course I did. I'm only delighted it takes your fancy."

"Are you sure you won't regret it?"

She picked it up and turned it round.

"Didn't you read the inscription? 'To regret nothing is the beginning of wisdom' "

"Do you think that's true?"

"Perfectly true." She laughed and added: "But impossible, I'm afraid."

"Perhaps if I have it always before my eyes, I shall learn to practise it," he said, taking out two notes. She raised a protesting hand and turned her face aside with a little shake of the head, as if to say she could not accept the money, at least not in such a direct manner. She seemed not to observe him lay the notes discreetly on the table; at any rate she made no further demur. When I walk out of here, I shall never see her again, he thought, as he slipped the plate into his case. His heart sank.

"Well…" he said, holding out his hand. "Goodbye."

"Goodbye," she said cheerfully. "Perhaps we shall meet again some day."

*

When she wrote to Rex to say, "Never again!" she had believed that when she went to him with the ten thousand, she would be able to persuade him to give up the rest of his plan. She had not counted on the extraordinary revolutionizing of her ideas when she actually held the cheque in her hand. She was swept over by an enormous excitement, a super-charged feeling of triumph and confidence. She wanted to turn cartwheels all down the street. She danced about the room, kissing the precious bit of paper, and flinging out her arms in extravagant gestures.

The next day, she paid in the cheque and told her bank manager that she had decided to buy a small country hotel she had found in the Cotswolds when she was away recently. It had been incompetently managed and in consequence the owner, a Birmingham businessman by the name of Jerome, was letting it go cheap to cut his losses. She had just received the surveyor's report and on the strength of it she had made up her mind.

She sent off a cheque for eight thousand pounds to Mr Jerome, and in the same week drew out the remainder and closed the account.

She mentioned nothing of this to her friends, and indeed up to the moment of her departure continued to fix luncheon engagements and dinner dates with them exactly as though she expected to keep them. And then without a word to anyone, she quietly vanished...

11

Life, says the old philosophical argument on Freewill and Predetermination, is like a game of chess, in which there are an infinite number of complex moves possible; the choice is open (that is Freewill), but the move contains within itself all future moves in the series right down to the conclusion of the game (that is Predetermination). That is, one is free to choose, but what follows is the result of one's choice. From the consequences of one's actions there is never any escape.

The first step in Rex's plan had now been brought to its conclusion. And already the long shadow of consequence fell across the future, reaching to that little stretch of woodland he had never seen, lying between Annecy and St Gervais-les-Bains, where he must eventually come to keep his grim appointment.

Part Two - "Blow The Man Down"
(Sea Shanty)

1

Leckenbridge lies some ten miles beyond Birmingham.

Before the war, it was no more than a tiny lost hamlet of five cottages; now it has become a smart neighborhood for prosperous middle-class businessmen and their families, with three-to five-bedroomed villas, each in its own acre, standing well back from the wide but unsurfaced roads. There is a golf course conveniently near, and a tennis club.

The Leckenbridge-ites are a sociable crowd, among themselves, that is. They like people "to join", if they are the right sort. In a small community, one has to be deadly careful to keep out the kind who don't fit. There had been, for instance, the dreadful Mrs Agnew, and the even more impossible little television comedian. The couple who had taken over the Fultons' place looked quite respectable, if dull. It was too early to say yet whether they would do. It never did to accept people in a hurry. One must first find out about them. Ticknell, the estate agent, told Roger Halcombe (who told his wife, who told the Wigmores, and so on) their name was Jerome and they had come from abroad.

*

During all the months he had to wait for Paula to join him, Rex had been searching for a certain man. He had tried to find him first in Manchester, then in Sheffield, then in Newcastle, but always in vain.

He had no idea who the man was or what he would turn out to be. He only knew that he must meet certain requirements: he must be well to do, between forty and fifty years of age, over six feet tall and heavily built, and preferably blue-eyed. In other words, without having to be his exact double, he had to resemble in general build and appearance, not Rex himself, but *Robert Jerome*. It was not as fantastic a search as it sounds, for Robert Jerome was still a vague indefinite figure subject to alteration. That is to say, Jerome could be made to look like *him*, once he had been found.

As Jerome, Rex frequented the sort of places where men congregate: pubs, businessmen's luncheon-rooms, political meetings, barbers' shops, football matches...

And then lunching one day in the restaurant of the White Hart Hotel, Birmingham, he saw him: a big balding man with half-rimmed spectacles.

Unless he turns out to have very short legs when he stands up, that's my man, Rex thought. When the waiter came over, he said casually, "You see those four men at that table on the left, do you happen to know the name of the gentleman in gray?"

"Mr Dexter, sir. Comes in here regular."

"Ah, is that who he is! I fancied he was a man I met in the South of France this summer."

"Oh yes, sir?"

There were, he discovered, eight Dexters in the phone book, so that hardly helped to identify him. The next evening, he entered the saloon bar of the White Hart, and as he ordered a drink, said to the barman:

"I'm looking for a Mr Dexter – a big chap about my height. I was told I might find him here. Do you know him?"

"That's right. He does come here, Mr Dexter. You'd find him here most weekdays about lunchtime. But he don't come in here often at this time of day."

Rex frowned and tsk'd his tongue against his teeth in annoyance.

"I have to get hold of him this evening. It's important. You don't happen to know where he lives, I suppose?"

"Can't say I do," said the barman, listening to the gentleman with one ear and taking in an order for three Tobys, a Scotch, and a gin-and-ginger with the other. He scooped up the wet coins and came back. "Connie might. Hang on a minute, she's serving in the Public."

"Now, don't rush me," said Connie, pressing a shapely finger to her temple to indicate thought. "He don't live in Birmingham, I know that for a fact... out in the country somewhere," she mused. "He had a rose he brought in... said he grows 'em... Leckenbridge. That's it! I knew I knew it."

So that was why Mr and Mrs Jerome went to live in Leckenbridge, to be near Charley Dexter.

It wasn't quite as simple as that of course. Houses did not often come on to the market at Leckenbridge. Nor did Rex want to have to buy the property, it would be a bore to have to tie up a large sum of money. The alternative would be to meet him in some other way. But though he might get acquainted with him, it still could prove a long and tiresome business to get himself invited to the house. And the whole success of his scheme depended on just that. On that, and Charley Dexter owning a passport.

Almost everyone possessed a passport in these days (even if one's business did not take one abroad, people had acquired the habit of going abroad for pleasure); but Rex could not afford to take any chances. Tickets are usually bought through a travel agency. It was only a matter of finding the right agency and putting the right question in the right way. Mr and Mrs Dexter, he learned, had made a tour of Yugoslavia four months ago.

And then by a piece of great good fortune some people called Fulton decided to let their house furnished for a year while they visited their son and grandchildren in Japan. Rex took it.

The Jeromes were set to begin.

They looked as different as possible from the careless bohemian Buchanans. The gay bearded giant in corduroys and jersey was transformed into a sober businessman in his mid-forties, dark-haired and clean-shaven. Paula wiped all the character from her appearance and made herself into a nice ordinary little woman wearing neat, good, tasteless clothes in heath colors and her hair knotted tidily at the nape of her neck. Her mobile expressive face became marvelously unresponsive, stolid, puddingy. Even her voice lost its husky thrilling overtones and took on a flat quacking note. This was the persona of Phyllis Jerome, dull, nice, unimaginative, unquestioning, thirty-two-year-old wife of Robert Jerome, retired tea planter.

One or two people called on them for subscriptions for this and that... the Horticultural Society, the local Conservative Group, the Music Circle meeting once a month for illustrated talks. Apart from that, no one talked to them. At the end of six weeks, they had got precisely nowhere. They had met no one. They were beginning to despair. The boredom was frightful.

And then just after Christmas, Anna Wigmore's corgi escaped from its mistress and dashed up the road, trailing its leash, to bark hysterically at Paula's unfamiliar ankles.

"Danny! ...Danny! ...Danny, come here!" called Mrs Wigmore. "It's all right, he won't hurt you, he's just showing off, the fool," she added, making a dive for the muddy lead. "You're a bad wicked animal," she informed him sternly, flicking the leash around his ears. The dog gave her a gratified smile and wriggled his hind quarters.

Paula stooped and patted his head, saying in the fulsome tones the English habitually employ to dogs:

"He's a good boy, yes he is, he's a good boy; he was only looking after his mother, wasn't he, yes he was."

She straightened up and the two women smiled at one another. Mrs Wigmore tucked in her fur-tie with a gloved hand and said pleasantly:

"You're Mrs Jerome, aren't you? I've been meaning to call on you, but I thought you ought to be allowed time to settle in before strangers began to descend on you. I wish you and your husband would come in for a drink one evening, I'd like you to meet some of your neighbors."

"That's awfully kind of you. We'd love to."

"Then let's make it next Thursday, shall we, about six? My name is Wigmore and we live at Fernlea – just down the road." And smiling, away she went, tugged along by the dog.

Paula turned back to the house.

"Darling, we've made it! We're in at last! I couldn't be more pleased with myself if the Queen had invited me to a Garden Party," she exclaimed, hugging him.

"Clever girl. I wonder if Dexter will be there."

"We'll soon get to know him now, don't worry."

"Do I ever worry?"

2

There were only half a dozen people there besides the Wigmores; the Halcombes, a man called Turner, a Miss Marksman, a couple by the name of Johnson; but not, alas, Charley Dexter or his missus. One gathered they did not quite belong to this set. A pity, but the Jeromes did not fail to make themselves agreeable on that account.

The field of conversation was small, ranging between washing-machines and fashion among the women, and golf and business among the men. It was a way of putting the Jeromes through an examination without direct questions.

Jerome let it be known that he had "come home" partly for reasons of his wife's health (the climate out there had not suited her), and partly to market an invention of his that, he said, would revolutionize the production of vegetable oil and thus immensely reduce the cost of soaps and margarines. The men were impressed. It seemed that he had discovered a new method of extracting oil from copra. Smart chap, they nodded among themselves.

At least it was a feasible tale and served his purpose by providing a good cover story to explain his comings and goings, and rendered a reasonable excuse why, although he did not appear particularly well-off, he had no place of business.

The following Sunday, returning to the club-house with Roger Halcombe after a round of golf, Rex saw in the bar, drinking with a group of men, the man he so much wanted to meet. And that was how he encountered Charley Dexter at last. It was no more than a casual golf-club acquaintance. Sometimes, after Jerome had become a member, they would find themselves drinking in the same company, or if none of Dexter's particular cronies had turned up they would play a round together. After one of these occasions he bought Dexter lunch at the club; a gesture of hospitality that Dexter accepted but did not bother to return. He was a negligent and busy man. Next, Jerome invited him and his wife over for drinks. This time the invitation was refused; they had a previous engagement. A month later, he asked him again. They came;

were pleasant, but did not stay long; and again nothing happened. It began to seem as if they would never get inside the Dexter home.

In April, he paid the second premium on the Jerome Life Policy, and shortly afterwards began to complain of dizziness and headaches.

"Hullo, taken to goggles?" said Ferdy Wigmore one evening in the Duke of York's. "They're new, aren't they?"

Rex touched the frame of his spectacles.

"These? Phyl thought my eyes might be the cause of the trouble, so I toddled off to see the eye chappie and he fixed me up with these. Horrible, aren't they? It'll be false teeth next."

"The old man's breaking up."

"That's it. Cheers!"

A few days later, he was playing a foursome, watching his partner, Ferdy Wigmore, addressing the ball, when he was seen to reel and fall to the ground. He lay there, staring up at them.

"Hey, what's the matter with you, old boy?" said Turner, helping him to his feet.

"Well, that was a funny go," he remarked with a sheepish air. "I turned giddy, must have lost my balance. Liver, I expect," he laughed, brushing himself down.

"Seen the medicine man about it?" Ferdy asked casually.

"Good lord, no. What next! He'd only tell me to cut out the drink or some rot like that."

"Why don't you have a word with Dr Parks," Ferdy said, as they strolled on, keeping his eyes on Turner hacking his way out of a bunker. "Might have a nasty accident if you had one of those blackouts while you were driving."

"Cheerful bloke, aren't you?"

And the next time he saw Ferdy, he said:

"I thought over what you said and I decided you were right, so I went to see some bloody quack in Brum, and it turned out exactly how I knew it would. The fool said it was blood-pressure and knocked me off the booze, and meat and fats and God knows what."

It was quite true that he had been to a doctor. Someone would be sure to check up on that after his "misadventure". Rex was always scrupulous about detail.

Phyllis Jerome called on the doctor too.

"I asked you to see me, Doctor, because I'm not altogether happy in my mind about my husband. His headaches and dizziness don't seem to be getting any less troublesome. I wondered whether—" she looked down at her handbag and ran a finger along its edge "—perhaps you had not told him the truth about his condition." She stole a quick glance at him and looked away again. (Mrs Jerome was the sort of person who is always too shy to look another in the face for more than a second).

"Why should I not have told him the truth?"

"If it was something very serious… incurable…"

"Such as, Mrs Jerome?"

She clicked the fastening on her bag open and closed.

"We had a dear friend, you see, who used to get terrible headaches and vertigo, and it turned out to be a tumor on the brain."

"And you're afraid that is what is the matter with your husband?"

She nodded dumbly.

He smiled benevolently.

"Then I can set your mind at ease, Mrs Jerome, your husband has no brain-tumor, I promise you, nor is there anything seriously wrong with him." He stood up.

"Really nothing serious? You're sure? I would rather know the truth."

"Quite sure, Mrs Jerome. There is a certain degree of hardening of the arteries. Nothing to worry about so long as he takes reasonable care."

"I see. And if he doesn't…?" she hazarded.

"Ah, then," he said with a shrug, and opened the door.

*

The Jeromes made a short trip to France in early July (at the same time that the Dexters were away), crossing Southampton-Le Havre in order to get a correct picture of the venue and make sure of the course to be traversed, to judge times and distance and choose the exact point for the final scene.

On their return, the Dexters gave one of their annual cocktail parties; one of those ghastly affairs that are a desperate attempt to wipe out old debts of hospitality, a melee of friends, acquaintances, and business contacts. Among those asked were the Jeromes.

There must have been some forty or fifty people wandering through the drawing-room to the paved terrace outside the french windows to stand, drink in hand, chattering like a flock of starlings.

Paula, captured by a talkative young man just back from Venice, signaled an appeal across the room with her eyes to Rex to rescue her. He came over and insinuated himself into the conversation so that Paula could escape. She drifted away.

It seemed most of the guests had arrived by now. This was her opportunity. The two maids were busy carrying trays of drinks and canapes. She walked out of the room and mounted the stairs.

The first door on the landing stood open. Someone had left a mink stole on the satin coverlet. Paula laid her handbag on the dressing-table and pulled out the bergere before it, as though – if anybody came in – she had been sitting on it. Against the wall facing the bed was a large satinwood wardrobe. She opened the right-hand door. Inside, shelves contained beautifully ordered piles of shirts and underwear. Taking care not to disturb their neatness, Paula slipped her hand beneath the garments on the first shelf, feeling for a thin stiff-covered book. Keeping her ear alert for footsteps muffled by the deep carpet outside, she drew out the small drawer under the shelf and explored among the collars and handkerchiefs, but it wasn't there either. Gently, she closed the drawer and shut the wardrobe door. She glanced around for another likely place (she dared not stay up here much longer) and was just trying the bedside table, when a faint musical humming caught her ear. She sprang away.

"Goodness, how you startled me!" laughed her hostess."

"Nothing to how you startled me," Paula said to herself, her heart thumping, and aloud said with her shy smile: "I've just broken my nail. I was looking for a file, I hope you don't mind."

"Oh, my dear, how maddening!"

"Yes, sickening…"

"…enjoying…?"

"…lovely…"

They exchanged the formal sprightly banalities, as Mrs Dexter ran a puff over her face and Mrs Jerome sawed the edge of her nail.

Seeing them descend the staircase together, Rex knew at once she had had no luck. Now it was up to him, and he would have to hurry, they could not stay much longer, people were beginning to leave; yet he must not be seen to disappear quite so soon after his wife's absence. He went into the garden.

"Anna, my dear, your glass is empty. Let me get you a drink."

"No, thanks, Robert, we're just leaving."

"Oh, not already! I haven't had a chance to speak to you all evening."

"Robert, I must. Tony's alone in the house."

Her husband came up and looped an arm through hers.

"Come on, old girl, let's go if we're going, for God's sake."

"You see?" Anna smiled at Rex, who held out his hands:

"Since there's no help, come let us kiss and part!"

"Here, none o' that!" said Ferdy, raising his elbow.

Rex went back to the house with them and when they had gone, walked away down the passage. He opened a door on the right... dining-room. Further down on the left was another door. This time there was no mistake. It was Charley's den sure enough. A flickering square of bluish light met his eyes. A glutinous voice said:

"...a *man's* smoke coo-ool and *satisfying*, in a *richer blend* than ever before..."

"Hullo, someone's playing truant," Rex said playfully.

Dexter put his head round the side of the chair.

"Jerome! Come in."

"No, I won't disturb you. I only looked in to say goodbye like a little gentleman."

"I suppose they're all beginning to leave, are they? I'd better make a smart effort to pull myself together and see them off," he said, standing up and stretching.

Rex was observing the lay-out of the room, noticing the position of the furniture, scanning the window-frame for bolts.

"I like your desk," he remarked casually. He strolled across to look at it more closely. "A lovely piece," he said, sliding the drawers in and out, as though to see if they ran smoothly on their gliders. At least they weren't locked, he thought in relief. "I've always wanted one of these kneehole jobs. Only one thing against them, as far as I can see: they don't build secret drawers in them."

"Ah ha, don't they, old man!" said Dexter, dealing him a hearty crack between the shoulders.

"Oh?" said Rex, with an air of innocent surprise. "Is there one in here?"

Dexter laid a finger against his nose slyly.

"Let me see if I can find it."

"Not likely," Dexter laughed.

"What do you keep there, dirty pictures?"

"That's it."

Laughing, the two men left the room. Rex could have bitten his tongue with frustration. His keen snatched glances into the drawers had been unrewarded by a glimpse of the passport. Another attempt would have to be made.

As they were saying goodbye, he said:

"Now, Mrs Dexter, when are you and your husband coming to have dinner with us?"

"Oh, that's terribly nice of you. We'd love to, sometime."

"How about next week?"

Mrs Dexter took a quick look at her husband.

"We're frightfully booked up *all* next week, aren't we, Charley."

"The week after, then," he persisted.

There are times when social resistance is clearly futile. The Jeromes would simply go on offering them date after date till they accepted; against their determination a refusal carried no weight.

An evening was agreed.

3

Six being a nice number for a dinner party, Rex invited the Wigmores as well, for the Dexters must not be allowed to feel bored or they might want to leave too early. The Halcombes were at least as entertaining as the Wigmores, but he chose the Wigmores for the simple reason that Ferdy only smoked a pipe and Anna did not smoke at all.

After dinner, as Paula was pouring the coffee, Rex, about to offer round cigarettes, found there were none in his case. The silver cigarette-box belonging to the Fultons was empty also.

"Phyl, haven't we any cigarettes?"

"I don't know, dear."

"Have one of these," said Dexter.

"I'm not going to smoke yours, my dear fellow. I'll trot down to the pub and get some, if you'll excuse me a moment."

"You don't want to bother to do that, Jerome. There are plenty here, plenty."

"But I don't want you to smoke your own. I wouldn't hear of it. I shan't be gone five minutes," he said with a gay little wave of the hand as he left the room.

He had a box of fifty in the glove compartment of the Morris, so there was no need for him to stop at the Duke of York's – which in any case was not on the direct route to Dexter's house.

He was there in three and a half minutes. Another half minute to put on gloves, draw a pair of black socks over his shoes for quietness and to avoid leaving tracks on the carpet, and he was soundlessly on his way, torch in hand.

There was a light over the front door and in the hall, and one lighted ground-floor window at the back of the house, from which came the blare of circus music broken with drum rolls… the servants watching the telly, he guessed. Nicer if the house had been empty, less anxiety.

On the other hand, it probably meant that the windows had not been locked yet for the night.

He walked round, looking for the study window. As he passed the back door, he gently pressed down the latch and felt it yield. He hesitated, just long enough to debate within himself whether he would be able to find his way to the study more swiftly through the unknown passages inside than by going round to the other side of the house to make an entry through the window, which might yet prove to be bolted. Opening the door a chink, he saw the passage was unlit and that decided him. He slipped softly past the light-rimmed door, from behind which came a bellow of multiple laughter, continued down the dark passage, almost bumping into a grandfather clock as he turned the corner, which sent his heart into his mouth, and groped along the wall for the first door on the right (he recollected it had been the last door on the left when he was approaching it from the other end).

The curtains were undrawn and there was just enough light for him to be able to see his way to the desk. The small direct beam of the torch shone into the first drawer. He pulled it out to its full extent, supporting the edge against his thigh, as he carefully lifted the contents. Not there... he tried the next one... and the one below that...

There were four drawers on each side and it took him more than two minutes to examine them. A burglar would have made a quicker job of it, tipping the contents recklessly on to the floor, but for him, the whole point of the exercise was that it should not be discovered. He had to effect a thorough search without disturbing anything. If it was suspected that the desk had been broken into, the absence of the passport would inevitably be noticed and then it would all have been in vain.

He was squatting over the last drawer when a sound leapt out of the stillness at him with terrible stridency, shocking him nearly out of his skin. He broke out in a sudden sweat. Which was not lessened by the realization a split-second later that it came from the telephone on the desk. He pushed back the drawer and stood up in a panic. There was probably more than one instrument in the house but this one might still be the nearest for the servant to answer. Its obstreperous call went on and on with impatient determination, as if the beast had life of its own.

He fancied he heard footsteps and darted to the french windows, kicking back the bolt with his foot as he turned the key. It wouldn't open. It shook in its frame but wouldn't open. It was stuck at the top. The sweat was running down behind his knees; he could hear his breath grunting audibly in his chest. And then he saw the bolt at the top and knocked it back. The door parted to let him out and was quietly closed. He crouched by the wall, waiting, frantic at the thought of every second wasted.

The telephone ceased at last its furious noise. After a moment, he went back into the room…

By the time, he got back to the house he had been gone close on twenty minutes. He bounced cheerily into the drawing-room, brandishing the box of cigarettes and full of apologies for his absence. Paula took a quick look at his face.

"You stopped for a drink," she said.

"Guilty!"

"I told you he had," she announced to the company at large.

"The fact is I ran into a bloke I used to know and I couldn't get away."

Anna, her eyes cast down in a demure smile, said:

"Robert, what *have* you got on your feet?"

Paula's heart gave a convulsive leap of terror as her eyes followed the direction of Anna's gaze and saw that Rex had forgotten to remove the black socks over his shoes. She tried to think of some light word that would rescue him, but her mind had gone blank.

Rex thrust out one foot and surveyed it with tolerant amusement.

"Well, get me!" he said. "Putting my shoes on before my socks and never noticing. Phyl, why don't you look after your husband properly? The poor fellow's getting past it, he'll be going out one of these days without his trousers, and that will really be the end."

There was laughter, and Ferdy said:

"I thought it was only brainy chaps like professors of philosophy who were absent-minded."

"That's where you're mistaken. My revered mother invariably left her gardening skirt under her evening dress when she changed for dinner."

"It runs in the family."

"Evidently."

Half an hour later, the Dexters rose to go and the party broke up.

Paula closed the front door and leaned back against it. "What an evening! I'm *exhausted*. Did you get it?"

"Yes."

"What kept you so long? I was going nearly demented," Paula said. "I thought something had gone wrong."

"I couldn't find the spring to the secret drawer, it had me nearly beat. I'm too old for this Commando stuff."

"Not you, you revel in it."

"I do rather," he admitted with a surprised air. "I like the feeling of being kept at full stretch."

"On the rack, you mean."

*

It was not very likely that Dexter was going to miss his passport until he needed it again. And he was not very likely to need it within the next three weeks. After that, it would be too late.

Jerome mentioned once or twice in pub talk that he was thinking of running over to France for a week or two. *Savon Cadum* appeared to be interested in his invention, he didn't know how serious they were but it seemed worth while to find out. Phyllis was going with him to help with the lingo, his acquaintance with Frog-talk being pretty meager.

Rex fixed the 27th of September for the trip, since one could count on a roughish passage during the autumn equinox. When he bought the tickets, he booked a first-class cabin for the night-crossing, Southampton-Le Havre. He took the trouble to go all the way to London for the purchase of the third ticket for the same journey; the third ticket being second class. And while he was in London, he bought a fawn tweed cap and a raincoat in reversible gaberdine, fawn one side and navy the other. For a few of those artistic touches he delighted in, he also bought some handkerchiefs monogrammed CD, an initialed studbox, and a pair of worn ivory-backed hairbrushes at a pawn-shop on which he had stamped the same letters. These articles were for the purpose of confirming his Charley Dexter identity if any inquisitive Customs Officer should choose to examine the contents of his suitcase. There would be three suitcases altogether, one for "Charley Dexter" and two for Mr and Mrs Jerome.

4

The 27th promised to be wet and windy.

Mr and Mrs Jerome traveled up to London by train. They dined together in Town and at 8.30 left for Waterloo in separate taxis.

A porter took the two Jerome suitcases from Paula and found her a window seat in the boat train. Presently, she saw Rex trudge down the platform with his heavy bag and climb into a second class carriage. He was wearing the fawn raincoat and cap, and the half-framed spectacles, like the ones Dexter wore, that he had got for his "headaches".

The slow rhythm of the train drawing into Southampton wakened Rex from his doze. He heaved his case from the rack and was first out of the compartment. He grabbed a passing porter to carry the bag to the Customs Shed.

The wind was fresh, the air moist, tasting salt on the lips. Deep black caves of shadow swung between the rocking lights, and as he passed out of the Customs Shed Rex said to his porter, "Meet you on board," and disappeared into the darkness.

When he caught up with Paula in the line of travelers shuffling towards the Emigration Officer with their passports he had become Robert Jerome once more, bareheaded and unspectacled, the raincoat folded on his arm, navy side out.

"Oh, there you are, darling," she said, handing him her passport, which he in turn passed over with his own for the Emigration Officer's inspection.

The officer glanced at Robert Jerome's passport and his wife's and gave them back with the Embarkation tickets.

Gusts of spray-laden wind blew across the quay, the stone underfoot was wet with past rain and slippery, running with streaked reflections. Vast murky clouds in the midnight darkness of the sky attacked the struggling slip of a moon like bravos of old, overpowering her and extinguishing her light.

As they mounted the gangway, an official at the foot collected from them their Embarkation tickets: *Robert Jerome had incontrovertibly gone aboard.*

Leaving Paula on the boat deck, he went down to the second class, assuming cap, glasses and raincoat in the Gents on the way, found the porter with "Dexter's" case and paid him off. He left the case in the second class saloon bar and strolled back on deck.

The siren hooted twice. There was a last swirl of activity, and the gangways were pulled away. The deck began to throb. He came and leaned on the rail beside his wife, watching the dark gap of water widen.

"Shall we have a drink before we turn in?"

"Yes, let's."

"I'll just cut along and see the purser about the cabin first. Meet you in the bar."

"All right, darling. Don't be long."

It must have been around 11.20 by the time his business with the purser was through and he joined his wife in the bar.

Shortly before midnight, as though to announce she had reached the offing, the boat dipped into a long shuddering roll. "Oh, dear," said Mrs Jerome with an unnerved look and stood up.

"Want to go up, dear?"

"I think so."

He steered her out with a hand beneath her elbow.

Five minutes later, the man in the fawn raincoat buttoned to his chin entered the second class saloon again.

"Getting a bit too fresh out there," he observed to the steward, blowing on his nails. He stayed there chatting desultorily to the steward and another man till a little after half past one, when he gave his glass a little push and said: "Mind that for me, I'll be back in a minute. Which way is it?"

The boat was pitching heavily and Rex had some ado to keep his feet as he lifted his suitcase on to the bunk and took out pyjamas, dressing-gown, and sponge bag. He left them in disorder on the bunk beside the open case, and began to empty his pockets: a handful of loose change, a pocket watch, his passport, folder of tickets, and wallet. He fastened the raincoat around his throat, navy side out.

"Ready?" he said.

"Ready," said Paula, hunched in her fur coat, looking very white.

"Valor, mujer!" Lightly, he dropped a kiss on her widow's peak.

She essayed a sick smile:

"Goodbye, Mr Jerome."

The doors leading to the deck were barred. Her arm in his, he marched her briskly, despite many a lurch, down the long corridor and back. A steward came towards them. Raising his voice above the elemental clatter, Rex said to his wife: "Feeling better, dear?"

She halted and drew a long unsteady breath.

"I wish we could get some air."

"It is stuffy," he agreed. "Steward, could we have those doors opened for a little while?"

"It's not advisable to go on deck, sir."

"No. If my wife could just stand in the doorway and get some air, she's not feeling too well."

"Very good, sir," the steward said, lifting the bars and pulling the door back on to its hook. The woman came to the threshold, the man steadying her with an arm about her waist.

"Ah, that's better!"

The steward disappeared, the corridor was empty: they slipped outside.

The moon had set; the night was impenetrably dark. The waters flung themselves against the sky in towering black steeps. The wind clapped like thunder. Every other minute, the boat shook itself in the air and plunged down again with a sickening drop.

With considerable difficulty, they fought their way aft along the wet slippery deck. There was no one in sight.

He had to put his mouth to her ear and scream the words: "The next time she gives a big roll!" He gave her elbow a fierce encouraging squeeze and left her, vanishing into the thick blackness... Now she was on her own.

The ship rolled, throwing her against the rail...

"*MAN OVERBOARD*!" she shrieked inaudibly into the storm, and ran staggering up the deck, the wind catching her screams and stuffing them back down her throat, whipping strands of wet hair into her eyes and across her lips.

The First Officer caught her in his arms as she reached the foot of the bridge. Her gasping lungs brought out: *"My husband... Back there..."* She flung out a hand.

The wind snatched the words away before they could reach him. He bent his face close.

"What?"

"*... HUSBA... OVERBOARD...*" he heard, and felt her tugging frantically at his sleeve.

There followed a tremendous confusion of whistles blowing... and shouts... and people running to and fro... the siren hooted... a flare on a lifeboat spun into the darkness and landed on the heaving waters...

*

In the second class saloon, the man in the fawn raincoat said: "Hullo, what's up?" as the engines went Full Astern.

*

For twenty minutes, the lifeboat they had lowered circled diligently around. It was hopeless of course. No man could stand a chance of survival in such a sea.

Mrs Jerome wouldn't leave the rail. Supported by a stewardess, she watched the lifeboat's flare bobbing into view and dipping out of sight again, growing smaller and smaller as it drifted away. Only when the engines were restarted could she be persuaded to let them lead her away. A doctor from among the passengers went with her. The poor woman was almost too distraught and incoherent to answer the distressing questions they were obliged to put to her.

"It was my fault... it was all my fault," she kept saying, "*I* made him go on deck: I wanted some air..." She wrung her hands.

"Could you describe what happened?"

"I don't know, I don't know... he slipped. I think he had one of his giddy turns... I saw him put his hand to his head... and then he fell... Oh God! Robert, Robert!"

"There, there," said the stewardess, patting her shoulder.

"I tried to catch hold of him... but the ship seemed to go right over on its side, and I fell against the rail... I saw this huge wave come up – I was terrified... and then it hit the deck – and – and – it must have dragged him..." She covered her face in her hands, shuddering.

(In this kind of situation you could act your head off freely. The more you sobbed and shook, the more likely. You really couldn't go wrong. It was a piece of pie. She wondered how soon someone would latch on to her remark about her husband's giddy turn; she didn't particularly want to have to bring it up again herself. And then she heard the Captain say:)

"You mentioned, madam, your husband having a 'giddy turn'. What makes you think that? Had he suffered that way before?"

She pressed her handkerchief to her lips.

"Yes… quite often lately. The doctor said it was blood pressure. He had terrible attacks of vertigo. He'd suddenly fall over. It used to frighten me." She blurted out a great sob, as though at the sudden realization of the past tense, and clutched convulsively at his dressing-gown lying on the bunk beside her, close to the pitiful small pile of objects he had left behind, like the pathetic little personal treasures found in an ancient tomb.

The doctor indicated discreetly that she was at the end of her resources and should not be questioned further. And indeed, there was small purpose in further interrogation. It seemed pretty clear what had happened. The Captain respectfully expressed his sympathy and left her to the ministrations of the doctor and stewardess.

*

A passenger lost at sea was a calamity that had never visited the Captain in the whole of his thirty years' service with the Line. A black mark on his unblemished record, with only three more years to go before he retired. He thought bitterly of the long unsatisfactory Inquiry, ending, no doubt, his gloomy experience told him, in vague and inconclusive hints of negligence.

"Well, Mr Jackson?" he grunted, as the First Officer joined him on the bridge.

"It seems pretty straightforward, sir. He joined the other first-class passengers in the purser's office as soon as we sailed. Purser says it must have been about quarter past eleven when he gave him his accommodation. That squares with Willis who saw him in Number One Saloon at twenty past with his wife. It was close on midnight when they left. In that time they only had one brandy a-piece. It was Browning who warned them not to go on deck. He had just come from the galley; he thinks it was about half past one. He says he noticed Mrs Jerome looked very pale and he heard Mr Jerome ask her if she was all right. She said she wished she could get some air, and he asked Browning to open the doors for them. That was when Browning warned them. But he latched back one door, and the last he saw of them they were standing together."

"And as soon as his back was turned they went on deck and ten minutes later he was washed overboard."

"It was a quarter to two when I left the bridge, sir, and she practically stumbled into my arms."

"What the hell were they doing walking round the deck for a quarter of an hour on a night like this with such seas running? You'd think he wanted to commit suicide."

"You're not serious, sir."

"Good God, Mr Jackson, of course I'm not," the Captain exploded. "A man doesn't suddenly decide to take his own life in the middle of undressing. Any more than he'd deliberately arrange to kill himself under his wife's eyes. Kindly don't make inane suggestions, Mr Jackson. I have enough to contend with."

Mr Jackson sighed. The Old Man had a stiff breeze up all right.

But there was this disagreeable little notion fidgeting uneasily at the back of the Captain's mind. The cases, he kept reminding himself sternly, were *not* similar: but he could not help recollecting that in 1932 there had been an instance of a married man who was believed to have disappeared on a Channel crossing. It was verifiable that he had boarded the boat, but from the moment she sailed, he was not seen again (although his absence was not remarked until they docked at Boulogne). It was presumed at first that he had gone overboard, but doubts were felt as certain information came to light. And in fact, the man was picked up by the police in Dornoch three weeks later. He had chosen this way of abandoning his wife and family, to start life afresh on his own. He pleaded amnesia, the charge was dropped, and he returned to his family. He had so nearly got away with it.

But no man would be such a fool as to attempt such a thing with his wife on board, with his wife actually *present*... no, it was out of the question.

5

The harbor authorities had to be notified and, what with the delay in mid-Channel, they were two hours late in disembarking. That too was a slow business, each passport carefully scrutinized, on the Captain's orders, each ticket checked.

The one thing that is hard to disguise is one's physique, particularly if it is big; a small man can make himself taller or stouter, but a large man cannot make himself small. There were three or four passengers on board of approximately the right build.

Rex came down the gangway among the second-class passengers, his cap tilted low, shadowing his bespectacled eyes, the collar of his raincoat up to his ears, the morning being decidedly chill.

He shifted his suitcase to his left hand, fished inside his coat, and handed over his ticket. It was in order.

He stepped aside at the bottom of the gangway and waited for the buxom elderly lady behind him. She was a Miss Cockpurse and she bred West Highland terriers.

Rex was saying to her as the French Customs official took the passport from him: "You tell them I sent you. Dexter's the name. Wait a minute, I'll give you my card." He took out his wallet and began looking through it.

"Oh, don't bother," said the woman.

"It's no bother, they'll be glad to help you," said Rex, apparently unconcerned by the attention the Customs officer was giving his passport. He had not even glanced his way.

"Pardon, m'sieu," said the officer.

Rex turned.

"Yes?"

The Frenchman looked at him for a second that to Rex was as long as that interminable moment before the fatal unavoidable impact in a road crash.

"Rien, m'sieu," he said with a polite little bow of the head as he held out the passport…

6

So it was over. Jerome was dead. At the bottom of the sea.

Dead? At the bottom of the sea? There was the rub! No body. And without a body, no inquest. Without an inquest, no proof of death. Without proof of death, the Insurance Company might baulk at admitting liability. They had to be *convinced*. For however much they may benevolently beam at one from advertisements, insurance companies are *not* philanthropic institutions. They will not pay out unless they are obliged to despite their cunningly-worded clauses. And yet, the one thing no company wants is to get a name for wriggling out of its obligations, that is too injurious to business. They aim at a reputation not only for paying-up but paying-up promptly without fuss. Orion Insurance was no different from the rest of them. They considered the claim would require investigation, and they instructed their Mr Marshall to look into the affair with all discretion.

The findings of the official Inquiry bv the Shipping Line were that Robert Jerome was "lost at sea, by misadventure" on the 28th September between 1:30 am and 2 am.

Mr Marshall studied the report with extreme care. There were one or two points that struck him as odd. The almost blatant abandonment of Jerome's personal belongings left in the cabin just before he went cn deck, for instance. As if he had wanted to stress the fact that they would never be needed again. Mr Marshall too was aware of the historical 1932 "disappearing act", but in this instance, the man's wife was on the scene. It didn't make sense. Unlike the other chap, Jerome had been seen on board after the boat sailed: there was plenty of evidence as to that. And how the devil could he have got off, with the whole crew on the look out for him? It just wasn't feasible. The correct number of tickets had been handed in at Le Havre – except for Jerome's, which had been found in his cabin together with his passport, keys and wallet. And once more Marshall found himself considering the significance of those discarded possessions...

Marshall stared abstractedly at the hexagonal design of minute black lozenges on a gray ground carpeting his hotel bedroom. It wouldn't work: it just would not work. From whichever angle Marshall approached the problem, the figure of Mrs Jerome stood in the way, making nonsense of the situation.

The irony was that he had his hand almost on it, if only he could have realized it. One tiny flaw prevented it, his judgment of criminal psychology. If a man wished to fake his disappearance, why run the risk of attempting it in front of his wife? How could anyone contrive a phony disappearance in such circumstances? It would not be possible.

That left suicide or murder. Again, the presence of the wife washed out the notion of suicide. Why should a man elect to kill himself while his wife watched? It would be cruel, hazardous and unnecessary. Altogether as improbable as the idea that she could have murdered him – a man turning the scales at fourteen stone pushed overboard by a woman barely half his weight! No, that one wouldn't wash! Nobody would be fool enough to attempt murder by that method.

He interviewed the stewards Browning and Willis, he interviewed Mr Jackson, the First Officer, but although he took them over their stories again and again, they told him nothing new. He asked for the names and addresses of any members of the crew who had not sailed with the Line before, and privately inquired into their histories, in case it might lead to some connection with Jerome. There was none.

In Birmingham, he visited the doctor who had attended Jerome and learned that it was perfectly correct that Jerome had been complaining of headaches and vertigo for some six months.

He talked with people who had known Jerome; Ferdy Wigmore and Roger Halcombe and William Turner, and heard about Jerome's invention and how he had but recently returned from Singapore (which fitted in with his Policy being of only eighteen months' duration). There were no unsavory rumors, no suggestion of his being interested in another woman, or of his wife being interested in another man; they were generally regarded as a respectable and quietly devoted couple.

He saw the widow. In a low apologetic, albeit determined, voice, he questioned her closely for two hours. She answered easily, without hesitation, except that once or twice she passed a hand across her brow and murmured: "It's all so confused now, I'm sorry."

"You say you went to your cabin just before midnight."

"Yes."

"And it was twenty to two when you and your husband went outside, is that right?"

"Yes."

"What were you doing all that time?"

She looked at him.

"Playing cards."

"Playing cards?"

"Yes."

"For an hour and – well, say an hour and a half anyway?"

"It was a bad crossing, Mr Marshall, and I'm not a very good sailor. My husband was trying to keep my mind off it."

"I see. And then at about half past one he started undressing for bed, is that it?"

"I became tired of playing and I wasn't feeling any better, so my husband suggested I lay down. I did, and then he started getting out his night-things. But lying "

"What happened to the cards? Do you remember?"

"The cards? I put them in my handbag. They were the pack I always carry with me when I'm traveling."

"Please go on, Mrs Jerome. I'm afraid I interrupted you. It was just a random thought because there were no cards found in the cabin. But of course there wouldn't be if they were in your handbag, I understand now. You were saying something about lying down, I think."

"I felt worse lying down. So I got up and said to my husband that I thought I'd walk about for a while. He said he'd come with me. I felt if only I could breathe some fresh air... I've told you all this before, Mr Marshall, need I go over it again?" she said with a trace of weariness.

"I'm sorry."

"What is there you still don't understand, Mr Marshall?"

"I haven't quite understood why you went outside after the steward had told you it was dangerous. Could you not get all the air you needed from the doorway?"

"I wanted movement, I felt better when I was moving." She leaned her head on her hand. "I'm sorry, I can't..."

"You've been very patient with me, Mrs Jerome, and I've taken up quite enough of your time," the man said, rising. There was nothing to go on, not one positive fact to indicate fraud. Suspicion alone is not enough: there must be motive and opportunity.

Marshall assembled his facts in a report for the Company; that was all he could do; the decision from the facts was theirs.

But by the time they had reached a decision, Mrs Jerome was no longer there to receive the money. A month after her husband's tragic death, she'd packed up and gone to stay with her sole living relative, a married sister living in Johannesburg. Mrs Jerome had left instructions with her solicitor for the ten thousand pounds to be paid into the Bank of South Africa to her sister, Mrs Brewster's, account.

It was done; and that concluded the Jerome affair.

Anna Wigmore received a picture postcard from Aden, promising a letter to follow. But the letter never came. And Mrs Jerome was never heard of again. Soon, she was forgotten.

Part Three - "A Tea Tray In The Sky"
(Mad Hatter's Song)

1

Durban was like Paradise after their stultifying middle-class life in the English provinces as Mr and Mrs Jerome. It was like some glorious fantasy of uninhibited wish-fulfilment in a land glowing with heat and color, with the private plane, the fabulous white Cadillac, the glittering white villa overlooking the bay with its marble swimming-pool lit from beneath and the padding black servants.

Scarcely a day passed without some mention of them in the Durban "Society" columns.

"Bartlemy Brewster and his lovely wife at the races (photo inset)."

"Lord Charles dancing with his hostess, the popular wife of tycoon 'Barty' Brewster,' and half a column about the famous Brewster parties.

"The 'Barty' Brewsters surf-riding with friends at Gold-berry Beach."

Blond, sun-bronzed and handsome, Rex was having the time of his life as Bartlemy Brewster, the larger-than-life tycoon. For a few short months, he was living in the extravagant spectacular style that only a millionaire could enjoy – but alas so seldom does!

It was in order to provide Brewster with the means to live like a millionaire for these brief months that Buchanan and Jerome had died their deaths. And this was to be the last great coup that would bring them in enough for ever.

Great wealth exerts a powerful charm on the mind. True, no one had heard of this mysterious financier prior to his arrival in Durban, but who would think of questioning his genuineness when his riches were so obvious and his hospitality on so lavish a scale?

The Brewsters were supposedly in Durban for a holiday. But among themselves, the men smiled quiet knowing smiles: that be blowed for a tale! He was up to something for sure. There must be some colossal deal in the offing, or why was he here? The chance of getting in on it (whatever *it* was) was too good to miss. They kept their ears and eyes open for a hint, for a clue, watching his least move, picking up every idle word he uttered and examining it for a possible ulterior meaning. So convinced were they by their own conjectures, that even his silences, his bland refusal ever to discuss finance or politics, they charged with significance. (Cagey birds these tycoons, giving nothing away!) Brewster was on to something, no two ways about it, or why did he make these mysterious solitary trips up-country in his own plane? Visiting friends, he *said*, and his wife disliked flying so he went alone.

The real purpose of these special journeys was to search out a suitable location for Bartlemy Brewster's flying disaster. Upon his arrival in Durban, he had taken out a "Personal Accident" Policy for flying only, insuring a capital payment of one hundred thousand pounds for his widow. A large sum, but not an immoderate one for a millionaire, whose sudden demise might precipitate financial crises in the several companies he owned.

It was no easy matter to find the exactly right spot for his proposed plane crash. Many factors had to be taken into consideration. The terrain had to be physically suitable. It had to be so isolated that there would be no chance of a witness. And yet, it had to be within march of some kind of civilization.

Meanwhile, there were other minor but not unimportant tasks to occupy his attention. The little matter of identifying the remains, for instance, in the event that the plane was ever found and if there were any remains left to identify. It would be best if Paula was not the only one able to identify these sad relics; Paula might be too ill from shock to undertake it! But with a little skillful direction of interest, anyone would remember a certain noticeable and characteristic ring that he always wore on his third finger; a ring, about which he narrated more than once a curious anecdote; a ring, to which he drew attention by playfully offering to give it to anyone who could get it off his finger. The ring was definitely a part of his identity.

That was easy. To procure a substitute for his body in the burnt-out plane was a trickier affair. A plane might be burnt to ashes and still traces of bones and teeth be found. Their absence might suggest at the least that the occupant had contrived to escape from the wreckage: and that would be disastrous. He had to safeguard against that happening by supplying a substitute cadaver.

Even if body-snatching was possible in this day and age, it was not practicable: one can't carry a corpse around in a hot climate. A ready-made skeleton was the next best thing. But even so not an object one can purchase just like that. Even at those establishments which supply medical students with the ghastly tools of their trade, the purchase would be noted – and remembered later if inquiries were made. Nor would it have solved the problem if Rex had bought one in England and brought it out with him: one can hardly travel with a skeleton in one's luggage, the Customs officials would be too surprised.

No, the only way to acquire one was through a medical student. And the first step towards that was to become acquainted with a medical student.

Now, medical students do not as a rule frequent the same social circles as millionaires; their youth and lack of means renders it unlikely. But somewhere among all the pretty girls that flocked around there must be one who had a brother or a boyfriend in the profession. But there again, one could not ask outright: "Do you know any medical students?" The information had to be acquired far more innocently than that. As when one of those charming creatures turned her mouth away from his lips.

"Don't you like me, darling?" he would gently murmur.

"Of course I do, Barty, I think you're sweet."

"But you don't want me to kiss you?"

"Oh, Barty, please!"

"What's the matter, darling? Have you got the 'jimmies' for somebody else, is that it?"

"The 'jimmies'! You are funny!"

"Come on, tell old Barty all about it."

For of course, there was always some tale to be told: the man was already married, or had gone away, or had not enough money... and "Barty" would listen sympathetically, continuing to feign an interest even after he had learned the man's occupation. It was a slow method, but not without its pleasurable moments.

One evening, he strolled into the garden with a girl called Sylvia, and as he stood with his arm round her, admiring the jacaranda tree in the moonlight, he picked up her ringless left hand and said with a quizzical smile: "How is it this little hand is bare? I should have thought an enchanting young thing like you would have been snatched up long ago."

She laughed.

"I won't let him buy a ring till he's passed his Finals: he can't afford it."

"Ah, so this astute old bird was right, there is someone. Who's the lucky he?"

"His name is Peter Rich."

"Well, let's hope that's an omen for his future. What's he going to be?"

"A doctor."

"Is he now!" he commented, giving her a delighted squeeze. "And why haven't I met him?"

"Oh, I don't know, Barty. He's always working. He studies frightfully hard, because we can't get married till he's taken his degree."

"And you want to get married?"

She smiled up at the pendulous plumes of blossom pale in the moonlight.

"Of course I do."

"Are you very much in love?"

"I am rather gooey about him."

"You must bring him up here. I'd like to meet him."

"Oh, Barty, it's awfully sweet of you, but I don't believe he'd come. He practically never has any free time."

"You tell him from me, work is all very well but life is for living. And I should know; I've worked damned hard in my time."

She flashed him a quick glance.

"The fact is – you mustn't be offended, Barty dear – but he doesn't like mill—" She caught her breath. "He doesn't approve of rich men. He's a radical."

"Of course he is. All intelligent men are. I tell you what, we'll have lunch together on neutral territory. Say, the day after tomorrow at the Royal Hotel; a modest inoffensive repast in the Cellar, tell him. I don't see that he can object to that, what do you think?"

"I think you're a dear," she said.

"Nothing of the kind. If this young man is good enough for you he must be well worth meeting."

2

Sylvia said, as they sat up at the Beach Bar drinking orange juice:

"I should have thought you'd be flattered that he should want to meet you."

"Why?" said the boy, opening wide his thickly fringed gray eyes.

"He is rather an important person, after all, darling."

"Important? In what way and to whom?"

"Oh, damn it all, Pete, can't you see how extraordinarily *nice* it is of him to bother?"

"Men like that are never just *nice*. He wants something from me – or maybe from you. Or else he *wouldn't* bother, you can take my word."

"Oh? And what have you got that a man like Barty would possibly want?"

He looked down into his glass, locking his fingers tightly through hers between the stools.

"You," he said huskily.

"Darling, you are so silly. If only you'd get rid of your obstinate prejudices for a moment, you'd realize how silly you're being. It can't do you any harm just to meet him."

"All right," he sighed.

She leaned close and rubbed her cheek affectionately against his.

"That's my good boy."

"I'd much rather be lunching with you alone."

"You'll like him, I promise."

*

The funny thing was she was right. Peter did like him. One would have to be a churl indeed not to like a person who so plainly was exerting himself to please. It is always flattering to be listened to and Mr Brewster had the additional charm of asking all the right intelligent questions. Moreover, when it is a millionaire who shows such interest, giving a rapt attention to one's words, it is difficult for an ordinarily modest young man, however radically-minded, not to feel flattered.

Sylvia sat between them smiling serenely. Now Peter could see how silly it was to be jealous. Now Barty could see how clever Peter was. Now she could drift off into dreams of her own while they indulged in their man talk...

They came up from the cool softly-lit Cellar into the shimmering brilliance and fierce heat of the street. They crossed Smith Street into the City Gardens, and sauntered past the crimson-throated lilies, the clumps of burning kniphofia and orange hibiscus and white chincherin-chees...

Rex said:

"I'd like to see over this hospital of yours. Could you show me round some time?"

"Be glad to."

"Good. I'll take you up on that," he promised.

A couple of days later, his Cadillac drew up outside the main block of the hospital buildings.

When the tour was completed, he said: "Highly instructive. I enjoyed that. And now I think we could both do with a drink."

Peter politely declined, saying that he had to get back to his digs and put in a couple of hours' study before dinner.

"All right. I'll run you home."

They drove across Durban to the back part of the city, a district of small Asiatic shops and shabby frame buildings, too near the native quarter ever to be "improved" or modernized. The streets petered out into unpaved roads, littered with fruit rinds and cigarette papers. A group of small black children squatted in the dust, throwing stones at an old can. An Indian woman shuffled by in a sari, carrying two hens upside down in a net. The natives who had been lounging on the sidewalk, ceased laughing and fell silent, regarding the splendid automobile furtively from the corners of their eyes, and then back at one another. Someone burst out in an explosion of tee-heeing mirth.

"Is this where you live?" Rex inquired with interest.

"A bit of a dump, isn't it? Well, thanks," he said, opening the door. "I'm afraid my room's in rather a mess or I'd ask you up."

Rex grinned.

"I was a student once upon a time myself: I haven't forgotten, and I don't suppose your place is any worse than mine."

"I warn you it's pretty squalid," Peter laughed, leading the way, since there was no help for it. He flung back a door: hastily kicked a shirt and a pair of socks out of sight under the divan, caught up an armful of books from the one easy chair and dropped them on the floor. "Do sit down. Can I tempt you to a glass of slightly lukewarm beer?"

Rex smiled vaguely as if he hadn't heard. As indeed, he hadn't. For he had seen it directly he entered the room; the object of all his endeavors, propped in the corner on its bony posteriors, a University gown draped around its clavicles and a tarboosh perched on its meerschaum-yellow cranium. His heart pounded with joy at this pleasant sight.

While Peter was rinsing a couple of glasses in the sink, Rex went across and examined it thoughtfully, deploying the joints in fresh arrangements.

"I like your chum," he observed as Peter returned with the beer. "What do you call him?"

"I don't think I call him anything," he replied dimly, cracking off the bottle tops.

"From the way you've dressed him up you seem to have given him quite a personality."

"Oh, that was just a couple of the chaps the other evening sending me up... cheers," he saia, handing "Barty" a glass.

Rex looked around for something to pin a new subject on and his quick eyes spied a German flute hanging by a string from a nail in the side of the cupboard.

"Hullo! You a musician?"

Peter shook his head from side to side.

"Nope. I wanted to be. But that's another story."

"A flautist?"

"Nothing less than a conductor."

"Really? What made you change your mind?"

He shrugged.

"The supply is greater than the demand, unfortunately."

"Too bad," Rex nodded sympathetically. "Still, it doesn't stop your enjoyment of music. You'll be going to hear Barbirolli at the City Hall next week, I suppose."

"Not a chance," the boy said gloomily. "I've been trying to get tickets for weeks; not a seat to be had."

Rex guided the conversation from music to Sylvia and presently said: "I must go, you want to get on with your work. Thanks for the beer."

On the point of leaving, he picked up the tarboosh, set it on his head, did a pirouette, and returned it to the skeleton's cranium.

"Peter," he said, as if struck by a sudden idea, "do me a favor."

"Sure."

"Lend me this old bod. I want to have a bit of a joke with him at a party. Can you spare him for a day or two?"

"Sure, sure."

Not for the first time Peter thought how dismaying it was that even a man as brilliant as Brewster must be could find amusement in a schoolboy prank. But perhaps, he reminded himself ruefully, it is better to be childish than a Prig.

Rex insisted he must come to the party and bring Sylvia; an invitation Peter politely if reluctantly accepted, thinking parties of all kinds – except the impromptu mess-ups in his digs – a bore.

But on the morning of the party, Rex telephoned him at the hospital.

"Look here, my dear boy, I've got a couple of seats for the Barbirolli concert tonight, and I wondered if you could use them. It seems a pity to waste them, and I remember you said you wanted to go."

"My God, I should just say I could! It's most frightfully good of you."

"Nonsense. There isn't anyone I'd rather give them to," said the other truthfully. "You can pick them up when you bring old Mustapha up here."

Now he had got the boy out of the way for the evening. It had been necessary to invite him in the first place, but he had no intention of allowing him to be present when the time came.

Two days later, Peter had a letter from him.

Dear Peter,

I'm afraid poor old Mustapha BA (failed) got broken up in a rough house the other night. I do apologize, and I hope the enclosed cheque will replace him adequately.

Yours,

B.B.

Peter's first impulse was to return the cheque. But second thoughts are best, and he decided to keep it. After all, he was a rich man and could afford to pay for his japes. It was really no concern of his that Peter no longer required a skeleton in his studies.

The conclusion satisfied both parties: Peter had a nice fat cheque, and Rex had his "body".

3

He and Paula waited a month before taking the final step.

Early on the chosen day, Paula drove him to the airfield. His plane was ready waiting on the tarmac of the private bay. A uniformed Bantu carried his cases across.

"Goodbye, darling," Paula said, kissing him. "Take care of yourself and don't be gone too long."

"I'll phone you. Have a good time while I'm away, and don't worry."

"I'll try not to."

The same last-minute conversation they always had. Mrs Brewster was always a little nervous, a little unhappy, on these occasions. It was well known that she disliked her husband flying; a natural apprehension.

"Don't wait, darling."

"I'll watch you take off."

He waved to her cheerily from behind the perspex. The engine came to life with a roar... the machine lumbered slowly forward... raced along the tarmac strip... skimmed the ground... rose smoothly into the air... diminished... and was lost to sight.

*

He phoned Paula from Pretoria that evening. The next morning before he took off again, he visited a small downtown barber's and had his blond hair clipped close in a Dutch cut.

*

He flew north-east, keeping the railway track on his right as a guide to his destination. Below him lay the illimitable scrub, like some mangy old lion's pelt, scarred here and there with dry watercourses, the dark patches of scrub looking like festering clusters of black flies on the faded brown skin.

*

The radio-operator in Ubompu control tower picked up his distress signals. They were very faint. He heard the pilot say something about engine trouble...

"Give me your position ... Give me your position."

A silence. And then:

"I'm going to try to land…"

"Give me your position… Give me your position…"

The remote tinny voice said:

"There's smoke coming from the port engine…"

"Can you give me your position… Give me your position. Reply…" repeated the operator urgently, pressing the earphones to his head as the sound faded. He just caught:

"…think… about fifty… south… Ingalele…" before it cut out altogether…

*

Rex did in fact make a fair landing on that uneven ground. And then began the slow sweating process under the sun's fierce blaze of dressing the skeleton in his clothes, adorning it with his personal jewelery, and rigging it into the pilot's seat. He changed his rich silk shirt and Florida suit for an old-fashioned cream alpaca and replaced the black sunglasses with a pair of blue tinted steel-framed spectacles. He settled a panama on his head, and surveyed his appearance as best he could in a pocket mirror. *"Du bist nicht schön, mein lieber Herr Schmid,"* the murmured with a grimace.

A few yards away from where the plane rested, the ground descended in a mild slope in a kind of shallow basin.

He leaned into the cockpit and started the engine, gave the propeller a swing, pulled away the chocks, and putting all his weight behind the wing trundled it into motion…

It gained a bumpy momentum on the incline… there was a crack as the propeller hit the rising ground. The nose tipped forward, and the tail lifted into the air, seemed to hang there for an instant, and then the whole machine fell heavily on its side, the wing crumpling with a rending sound…

He waited, heart in mouth, till he saw a pale crocus of flame flower on the bodywork… The noise of the explosion when it came seemed to crack open the vast silent sky itself, hitting the watcher like a physical blow. A ladder of flame shot heavenwards, trailing a stream of black smoke across its pure azure. Fire enveloped the entire plane with a tearing sound. The blaze created a heat so intense that the landscape shimmered as if it stood behind a wall of glass running with water…

Bartlemy Brewster had joined Robert Jerome and Rex Buchanan in the shades...

Herr Schmidt picked up his case and began his trek towards the distant railway line which would guide him eventually to Ingalele; the next stop on his long route to an unknown destination and the rendezvous he was going to keep with Murder somewhere between Annecy and St Gervais-les-Bains.

Part Four - "Whither Will You Wander"
(Nursery Ditty)

1

Slender and elegant in the black and white Balenciaga cotton and large shady hat, she crossed the sun-dappled *Place* to a pavement-table at the café on the corner to wait for Rex to complete his business at the bank.

She lit a cigarette. It was a heavenly day; she felt as light as a bird now that the long intolerable strain was over at last. No more need to be ever on guard, the ordeal was ended. They had only arrived in Geneva the previous day and just as soon as the Guatemalan visas came through for "Mr and Mrs Ross Vanbrugh" they would be off to Central America to live the rest of their lives in the peace of a country where the extradition laws did not apply. Already the delightful sense of freedom gave her an absurd desire to smile at everyone.

Somebody stood between her and the sun, casting a shadow across the café table. She looked up, thinking it was the waiter come for her order.

A tall young man gazed down at her, his handsome Spanish-oval face shaded by the brim of his hat. He lifted it off and smiled at her warmly.

"*Hullo!*" he said. "What a wonderful piece of luck running into you like this. I was almost afraid it couldn't really be you, it seemed too good to be true."

For a moment, she thought it was just a pick-up, but he had addressed her in English, indeed was English himself; a Frenchman would approach a woman of her type, but not an Englishman – mischievous, innocent, little girls were what Englishmen went for. Besides, she had the impression that they must have met somewhere at some time, she felt she had seen him before, there was something vaguely familiar about his face which she could not quite place. So she gave a faint smile and said:

"Have we met before? I'm afraid I don't remember."

A childish look of disappointment fell across his countenance.

"There's really no reason why you should, I suppose. It was a long time ago. But I could never forget you, Mrs Buchanan."

The huge black sunglasses continued to stare up at him expressionlessly, but the shock of hearing that name had chilled her as though a cloud had passed across the sun. She tried to collect herself and think what to do. She tried desperately to remember who he was. If he had known her in the old days, it was more than likely he had known Rex too. And any moment now, Rex might come sauntering down the street. And then what would happen? One thing was certain, *he must not see Rex.*

"May I?" the young man was asking politely, drawing out a chair as the waiter approached their table. "What will you have?"

"A Campari. Will you order it for me; I'll be back in a minute." She walked swiftly into the café. Not to return to him might be dangerous, but she had already decided that was what she must do if she could not get hold of Rex.

She found the bank number and got through.

Mr Vanbrugh, they said, had just left the building.

"Could you please try to catch him, it's terribly important. This is Mrs Vanbrugh." She hung on, waiting, watching the young man's back through the plate glass window. Rex came to the phone.

"Listen," she said. "Don't pick me up, go straight back to the hotel. I've run into someone who knew me in London."

"Who?"

"I don't know. But I'm going to find out. I don't remember him, but he remembers me all right. That doesn't matter so long as he doesn't see you."

"Take care," he said, as she rang off.

She sat smoothly down beside the young man and smiled at him sweetly over her glass.

"Well now, tell me all about yourself, Mr – er – I'm afraid I've forgotten your name, do forgive me."

"It's Maddox – Stephen Maddox."

"Of course. And are you enjoying yourself in Geneva?"

"I am now," he said with a glance of smiling candor. "I've so often hoped I should see you again. And then to run into you here of all places! It's extraordinary, isn't it, the way one always seems to meet people one knows abroad?"

"You're on holiday, I suppose."

"Well… yes… in a way."

"In a way? How mysterious," she laughed. "What can you mean? Are you staying here long… 'in a way'?"

105

"I don't know. Are you?"

"I don't know. So there!" she countered blithely.

He burst out laughing.

"I don't need to ask how you are; you're looking marvelous," he said, eyeing her with frank admiration, from her polished bronze shoulders to her mouth as red as the ruby the size of a postage stamp glowing on the hand that rested on her white buckskin handbag. "But what have you been doing all this while?"

"Ohhh… enjoying life, you know. And you?"

"Oh me, I'm still in the same old job with the same old firm," he shrugged, poking at the little cardboard beer mat with a curious air of discomfort.

"And what was that? Or should I remember?" she asked lightly. For the wretched man obstinately refused her all clues. One might almost think it was deliberate. But that of course was merely her nervous imagination.

He was looking at her in blank astonishment.

"Have I said something frightfully stupid?" she said with a nervous laugh.

He gave her the strangest smile.

"Nevermind," he said.

The Cathedral clock scattered its chime across the town. "Good heavens!" Paula glanced at her watch and jumped up. "I'd no idea it was so late. I must fly."

"Oh, wait!" he said. "I shall see you again, won't I?"

"Oh, I'm sure you will," she said easily.

"Would you – have dinner with me one night?"

"I won't promise," she smiled, withdrawing her hand from his clasp, and threaded her way quickly across the street.

*

"He came up to me while I was sitting outside the café waiting for you," she told Rex when she got back to the hotel. "Honestly, darling, it was like a cold hand gripping the back of my neck when he called me Mrs Buchanan. I didn't know what to do. I thought the best thing was to stall along and try and find out where we met."

"Did he say anything about me?"

"No, actually I don't think he mentioned your name."

"Do you think he knew you were a widow?"

"I've no idea."

"You didn't tell him you had married again."

"Of course not. Supposing he sees you somewhere and recognizes you."

"He won't do that. We're not going to give him the chance; we're leaving here now. The bill is paid. The bags are packed."

"Where are we going?"

"We'll see. The thing to do is to get going, we can decide where to stop when we get there."

"And the visas?"

"We'll pick them up later. We can't wait here till they come through, that's for sure."

"You don't think you're making rather too much of this, my pet?"

"Why take unnecessary risks, my dear? 'Better,' my old nanny used to say, 'be safe than sorry'."

"There's a belated piece of wisdom, if ever I heard it."

"Well, if you could only remember who the fellow is," Rex answered, ringing for the pageboy to carry down their luggage.

"I wish I could. There was something familiar about him. It keeps bothering me. I've seen him somewhere."

*

They stopped in Berne for lunch. It was during the meal that Paula suddenly laid down her fork, leaned her brow on her palm, and muttered faintly: "My God!"

"What's the matter?"

"It's come back to me. I know who he is. Oh Lord, how could I have forgotten! No wonder, oh no wonder he gave me such a peculiar look when he told me he was still in the same old job and I asked him what it was. He expected me to know. Of course he expected me to remember that much about him if I had really recognized him as I pretended…"

"Could you be a little more lucid, dear?"

She swallowed some wine.

"He was the man from the Insurance Company who came to pay over the money."

"Rather odd of him to bring himself to your notice again, in the circumstances, don't you think? I wonder why," Rex pondered, frowning. "A pretty cheeky thing to do."

"Well, hardly tactful perhaps – I suppose that's why he didn't like to remind me – but I'm sure he didn't mean to be impertinent. He was just terribly pleased to see me. I think he was feeling lonely and it cheered him up to see someone he knew, however slightly."

"Oh, come off it, Poll!"

"What's so surprising about that?"

"Did.he want to see you again?"

"Of course he did, poor young man."

"Lick the cream off your whiskers, my dear; I hope you're justified in that smug look; I should hate to think he was concealing some other and more sinister purpose behind his gallantry."

"Don't be so stuffy, darling. You just can't bear anyone to make a pass at me."

"I can think of worse things even than that," he said, signaling for the bill. "At all events, he knows you're widowed, and he can't ever have seen me – he'd be working in a different department. Unless," he added, struck by a sudden thought, "he saw a photograph of me at the flat. Could he have?"

"I don't know. You can't expect me to remember whether there was a photo of you lying around, after two years. Do be reasonable. And anyway, what does it matter now? We're not likely to run into him twice. That would be too much of a coincidence."

"You're so right, my blossom. I was only wondering how a pay-clerk in an insurance office could afford a holiday in Switzerland... if it is a holiday."

Paula was silent, recalling the embarrassed tone in which Maddox had said, "...in a *way*..."

"Did he tell you how long he was staying?"

"No-o-o-o. He would hardly speak about himself at all. I don't know which of us was the cagier," she laughed.

"Really," Rex said thoughtfully, heading the car towards the Canton of Zurich. "Perhaps he didn't want to commit himself till he knew how long you would be staying."

"Could we forget him and talk of something else for a bit," Paula said plaintively.

*

On the evening of their second day in Zurich, Rex was sitting in the St Gotthard Hotel bar, talking to an Englishman who had just arrived, while he waited for Paula to finish dressing for dinner.

The Englishman was describing his route, when he broke off in mid-sentence, staring past Rex's shoulder with a startled look on his face.

Intrigued, Rex turned to see what had aroused this vivid reaction.

"Ah," he said, rising to his feet, "there you are, darling."

She seemed to hesitate a moment where she stood in the entrance, and then rustled slowly across, her face pale beneath the somber lighting.

"You must meet my wife," Rex said. And taking her arm, added, "Paula, dear, this is Mr Maddox."

"We have met already," said Paula. "Extraordinary the way one keeps meeting people one knows abroad, isn't it?"

*

"Why the hell did you never tell me the fellow's name was Maddox?" Rex said angrily, pulling off his tie, some hours later.

"I thought I had," Paula shrugged. "What difference would it have made anyway?"

"Oh, don't be dense. I'd have warned you not to come down. He had no idea who I was, I'm dead certain of that."

"You'd have been able to have some jolly times together, no doubt, while I was locked up in the attic like Bertha Rochester," she remarked, smiling at herself coldly in the mirror as she unscrewed her earrings. "And how long were you proposing to keep me shut up, dear?"

"Please, don't be irritating. We'd have left later tonight, of course."

"We still could."

"No. Not now." He bent down to wrestle with a knotted shoelace. "Now we've got to find out what he knows."

"About us, you mean?" She opened her jewel case and fitted the earrings into their velvet grooves. She unfastened her diamond watch and the brooch at her breast. "I don't see how he can know anything."

The shoelace broke, and he swore, wrenching off the shoe. He straightened up, his face darkly flushed.

"You think it's just coincidence that two days after meeting you in Geneva, he turns up here in Zurich at the same hotel?"

"Not necessarily a coincidence. He may be here on my account without it involving you in any way. Don't forget that until this evening he didn't know of Ross Vanbrugh's existence. Probably he regarded me as a desirable rich widow, and if he did follow me here, I dare say that was why."

"My gal's so modest…" hummed Rex. He came and stood behind her, watching her in the mirror with a smile. Slipping a hand beneath her chin, he turned her face up to his. "I only wonder where he gets the money to stay at the St Gotthard."

"Unzip me, please."

He caught hold of the little tab; the dress split open like the dark sepals enclosing a white flower. It fell about her feet and as she stepped out of it, she said:

"You think he's been sent out here by his firm, all expenses paid, to find us and… discover the truth."

"Don't you?"

"I don't know. He seems so gentle, so…"

"Would you expect him to come up and lay a heavy hand on your shoulder like a dick?"

"I don't see how he could have known we were coming to Switzerland."

"Baby, you have to realize that they may have been on our trail for a long time."

She shivered, hugging her arms across her breast.

"Why should they? What can have gone wrong?"

"There was always the chance that something might come to light over those cremation forms eventually. That some time the doctors would discover that neither of them had in fact examined the corpse. That would involve *them* in a felony. It doesn't involve us. Not yet. No one can prove there never was a body. And without proof there's nothing anyone can do."

"And you believe that's what he's after." She wiped her face with a pad of cotton wool, regarding her image steadily. "Rex, why don't we leave now – at once."

"Because, darling, I don't propose to spend the rest of my life skidding away from danger. I want to know just where I stand."

"What are you going to do then?"

"We're going to be very nice to this young man, very friendly. We'll stick to him closer than a brother. He'll be astonished at his own luck. But sooner or later he'll give himself away."

"And if he doesn't?"

"Then I'll know I was mistaken, and that will be that."

"But if you're *right*, what then?"

"Time enough to decide that when we know." He slid a hand over her smooth shoulder. "Not to worry, my love, Daddy-oh's here."

Paula locked the jewel-case in the table-drawer between their two beds and tucked the key beneath her pillow. Apart from a few thousand pounds in a joint drawing-account in the Bank of Switzerland, their entire fortune was contained in that small leather box.

Really costly precious stones in fine settings will always fetch their value (the diamond parure alone was worth sixty thousand pounds). And personal jewelery is the most easily transportable form of wealth from one country to another. It was, needless to say, fully insured, but she guarded it with the greatest care. By day, the case was always deposited in the hotel safe, and when travelling she carried it in her hand. They were taking no chances.

*

Rex leaned over the table where the young man sat at breakfast.

"We're going to Lucerne for the day. We wondered whether you'd like to come with us – if you've nothing better to do?"

Stephen Maddox looked up and flushed in surprise.

"That's awfully nice of you." He hesitated, biting his lip. "If you're sure you want me, I'd love to come."

"Good! Meet you in the foyer at half-past ten."

Maddox remained for some minutes with bowed head, staring fixedly down at his finger ends.

If you had a grain of common sense or even a spark of decency you'd leave here right away, he told himself. Can't you see they're nice people – both of them? He pushed away his plate and lit a cigarette. I could tell him I've changed my mind, make some excuse…

"The gentleman has finished?" inquired the waiter, hovering at his side.

"Yes." He dropped the crumpled napkin on the table and stood up. His hesitation came suddenly to an end. He said hurriedly: "Oh, by the way, I shan't be in for lunch."

"No, sir," agreed the waiter. "Herr Vanbrugh has already the information given."

*

It was a glorious day, sparkling with sunshine and laughter, like the waters of the lake. Paula insisted on driving on to Küssnacht, fascinated by the name ("God knows what she imagines she's going to see!" said Rex), and they lunched there in a garden restaurant, which looked down on the dancing blue waters below.

"And tomorrow where shall we go?" Paula asked dreamily, turning her face to the sun and closing her eyes.

"Basle," said Rex.

"Unter Walden," Paula said.

"Basle."

"Unter Walden," Paula repeated sweetly.

"Darling, it means covering the same route we've taken today."

"Does that matter? It's very beautiful. And what's so special about Basle anyway? We can go there another time."

"Where would Stephen like to go?" Rex asked, smiling at the young man. "He's our guest."

Stephen looked from one to the other uncertainly.

"You really don't have to… I mean," he stammered, "I rather thought tomorrow I'd go off and explore the—"

"No, no, no. You're coming with us," Rex said firmly.

Paula said:

"You mustn't bully him, darling. He may prefer to be by himself."

"Piffle! No one wants to be alone on holiday. You can't have any fun by yourself. That's absurd. It's just that he thinks he's *de trop*, the silly ass. Of course he's coming."

"Well, that's that," said Paula, confiding Stephen an amused glance, as Rex strolled away up the winding path to the *Gasthaus* to pay the bill.

"It's extremely kind of your husband," Stephen said uncomfortably. "I don't know why he should bother about me."

"Oh, Ross likes to have people around, he has a gregarious nature. But if you'd really rather not come, I'll put it right with him later."

Their eyes met.

"I would like to," he said, feeling horribly ashamed of himself. "Of course I'd like to. So long as I'm not in your way."

It seemed a long moment before she answered, her gaze still holding his with a mutely-questioning look. And then she said:

"Don't be absurd; we both want you."

We interpret the world about us through our own hopes and fears. The words that others speak we hear as the answers to our thoughts. In dread or desire, we look for what we expect to see, and are led ever deeper into the toils of our own making. So Stephen read into the question in Paula's eyes the response to his own feelings; whereas Paula, between fear and doubt, made of his hesitations a reluctance for treachery; and Rex, caught in the web of his guilt, saw in him the sly silent hunter, forerunner of Justice. None could see the other divorced from these personal emotions. The three of them were binding themselves together inextricably with the unbreakable bonds of their own beliefs.

2

They left Rex at the Basle Offizielles Verkehrsbvero and sauntered in the pleasant midday warmth through the Freiestrasse to the Kunstmuseum. Leaning on the embankment, watching the river flowing swiftly past, and talking of this and that, Paula contrived to slip in some casual comment about his being able to afford a holiday in Switzerland.

"Oh, the firm's paying," he said easily.

Her heart thumped in her breast. She looked up at the swaying roof of leaves patched with blue, drawing deep breaths to steady herself.

"Then this isn't just a holiday?" she managed to say with an air of idle interest.

"Well – not exactly."

"And what does that mean?" she laughed.

"As a matter of fact," he said, with a shade of hesitation, and he gave a nervous laugh, "I'm supposed to be on sick leave."

"Really?" she said, and there was the merest hint of incredulity in her tone. "You look all right."

"Oh, I am, perfectly," he assured her. "But don't tell them I said so." Better to joke about it than bring up sour memories of his months in hospital and spoil the bright day. He was not to know how improbable his words sounded in her ears, or that for her the bright day was spoiled indeed. But something, he noticed, was wrong, she had fallen suddenly quiet, and he asked her what was the matter.

"I was wondering where Ross had got to."

"Here he comes now," Stephen said, pointing in the direction of the Cathedral. And as they watched him approach, he remarked oddly: "I like him so much, you know."

"Do you? I'm glad."

He turned: they were very close. His dark shadowed eyes looked sadly down at her.

"I wish I didn't," he said in a quiet strange voice. For what can be more terrible than to like the husband of the woman you're in love with?

To Paula, his words meant clearly a regret that he should be committed to betraying a man he liked. She tried to laugh, to say, "What an extraordinary remark to make!"; but she couldn't, her voice failed her.

"Well, what are you two looking so glum about?" cried Rex, clapping them on the shoulders. He saw fear in Paula's eyes. He said gaily: "I don't know about you, but I can't face trudging round looking at a lot of art without a little encouragement. Let's leave the old Kunstmuseum till we've had a drink or two."

"I'm right behind you," said Stephen, laughing. He put a hand in his jacket pocket, letting them walk ahead. "Hey!" he called. And as they turned, he raised to his eye a miniature Rolleiflex. "Say 'cheese'!" he grinned, clicking away rapidly. "Come on, Ross, let's see those gorgeous teeth, this isn't a passport photograph."

"You dirty dog!" laughed Rex, assuming a joviality he was far from feeling. His fingers locked through Paula's with so fierce a grip that the pain nearly forced a cry from her lips. It was immediately obvious to him why Stephen Maddox was taking these snapshots. He wanted a photograph of Ross Vanbrugh to send to his firm in London for comparison with any existing records of Rex Buchanan. It was the one essential link, the *proof* of fraud. Stephen had trapped him with exemplary skill and cunning. He fought to master an overpowering anger, to subdue the impulse to rush at him and trample the camera underfoot.

"Now, Paula alone," Stephen was saying. "On the Cathedral steps, I think… looking up at that old stone saint… that's perfect…" He glanced back at the sun, and shifted his position, choosing his angle with great care.

"Are we going to have that drink or not?" Rex said im-patiently.

"Just one more of you, Ross. Please!"

And Rex, on the point of turning away with a sharp refusal, changed his mind and, smiling, struck a magnificently virile pose. But as Stephen's fingers moved to the button, Rex threw up his hand before his face, jerking his head back, as though to thrust off some alarming insect.

Stephen gave an exclamation of annoyance.

"Ross, you moved!"

"Sorry. I think you got me all right."

"Do keep still this time, I've only one left," he said, backing away as Rex came towards him.

"Then I claim it," Rex said amiably, taking the camera from him. "I must have one of you and Paula. Now, where…" he mused, looking round. "Standing on that old bridge, I think, would make a good picture." He stood at the foot of the bridge, watching them turn midway up the slope, arm linked in arm. He considered them, his head on one side, dodging back and forth with a dissatisfied expression. He raised the viewfinder to his eye, and shook his head. "No… I tell you what: you go and perch on the embankment, Paula, with Steve beside you, and I'll shoot it from the middle of the bridge, I want to get an interesting composition."

They looked at one another with a sigh and a shrug, and obeyed.

"How to be happy though married," said Paula, hitching herself up on to the sunbaked stone.

Stephen placed an arm around her just below the waist, to hold her safe. A gesture performed in all innocence, out of tenderness and protection. He could feel the warmth of her flesh through the thin cotton, the supple spring of her spine rising from the delicious curve of her hips; and the sensation gave him a strange breathless anguish behind his breastbone; his knees shook, and his mouth was suddenly dry. Paula could not draw her eyes away from his, her own large with alarm at the trembling that had seized her. The sudden desire to press her mouth upon those full firm lips made her dizzy.

"That's fine!" Rex shouted from above. "Turn your head a little more this way, Poll." He hoisted himself higher, lodging his feet between the pilasters and hanging over the parapet of the bridge. "Smile, can't you?" he adjured them, the camera cupped to his eye. He wriggled an inch or two further along, still looking through the viewfinder, and as he did so, contrived somehow to strike his elbow sharply against the edge of the parapet, sending the camera flying out of his hand. He gave a cry of dismay as it fell through the air and sank with only the faintest splash into the rushing waters below… that had disposed of that, he thought thankfully, running down to meet the others with profuse apologies. The photos of Ross Vanbrugh were gone for good, and he'd see to it there were no others.

"My dear fellow, how can you ever forgive me! I don't know how I could have been so clumsy. You must allow me to replace it of course."

"It doesn't matter," Stephen muttered, almost as if he was thinking of something else. He seemed dazed.

It's jolted him, Rex thought, it's given him a bad jolt, he was really counting on those photos.

"We'll get you the finest Zurich can provide," he assured him (thus, subtly postponing the purchase to another day).

Stephen took it quietly. He protested no more, but there were moments during the rest of the day when some inner preoccupation held him in profound silence. Paula, on the other hand, assumed a brittle nervous gaiety like a high-strung hostess trying to make a party go. And all the while beneath his cheerful front, Rex was wondering just how much Stephen knew or guessed about them, and what thoughts were working for their destruction behind that smooth brow.

He had managed for the time being to prevent him getting a photograph, but that only provided them with a temporary respite. Stephen would not be put off so easily from accomplishing his task. With or without a photograph, he would no doubt find a way to get his facts. Rack his brains how he would, Rex could not fathom a way to stop him. Recalling wryly the old Russian proverb, "Who rides on a tiger cannot dismount," Rex began to wish he had not stayed to engage in this duel of wits. It might, after all, have been wiser to have fled at once, the night Maddox turned up at the St Gotthard. He had been held back from flight by his overweening self-confidence that could not believe he was not more than a match for any man living. Had he not proved his superior intelligence again and again? The excitement of pitting his mind against the unseen moves of another was a temptation he could not resist. And so he had stayed, and only now was he beginning to regret it.

But he was never one to capitulate; even to himself he would never acknowledge fear – fear was weakness. Instead, with typical *braggadocio*, he boasted of his quickwittedness to Paula, when they got back to the hotel and were alone once more. But for some reason, Paula did not give him her usual response. She seemed quiet and preoccupied.

She was in great confusion of mind. She did not know what to think. And she was afraid. Running against the words: "A sort of holiday… The firm's paying… I'm supposed to be on sick leave… I like your husband so much; I wish I didn't," was the remembrance of his yearning glances and the shock of his touch.

"I admit it gave me a nasty moment when I turned and saw him with that blasted camera," Rex was saying. "Considering how nearly he had me, I venture to think I handled it pretty neatly."

"Yes."

"Yes! Is that all you can say? If I hadn't acted so promptly, my dear girl, that pernicious little roll of film might be on its way to London by now."

"I wonder if that was what he was going to do with it, or whether he just wanted the pictures as a memento of two people he thinks of as friends."

"My dear Poll, aren't you being a trifle naïve?"

"Perhaps."

"You have only to consider the way he went about it, to realize his motives. He deliberately took us by surprise because he was bloody well determined to get a picture of me, and he was afraid that if he asked me outright I might make a fuss."

"You may be right." She bent to pull off her sharp-heeled shoes. "But if you are, he won't be as easily defeated as that. He'll find some other way to get a photograph of you, if that's what he's really after."

"So? I shall find a way to prevent him succeeding. It's as simple as that."

"Is it? I wonder."

He said angrily:

"What the hell's the matter with you all of a sudden! Don't you think I'm a match for that commonplace boy?"

Too much of a match, she thought, and that's what hurts. For whereas she could not bear to think that Stephen was exploiting them in this cruel game, Rex had become so obsessed by his own trickery that he could no longer credit innocence and sincerity to anyone: his mind was self-corrupted. She thought bitterly, as she sat on the edge of the bed and slowly peeled off her shadowy nylons: Soon, he won't even trust me. She gave a little shiver. This was the price they had to pay, they could never trust any other person ever again.

Rex came and sat beside her, slipping a hand with easy habitude inside the wide neck of her frock.

118

"Listen. I know how you feel, doll-baby. But you mustn't get sentimental about this young man just because he's a little in love with you. There's only one thing to remember: that if he has his way he can get us fourteen years. I'm not saying that he wants to, or even knows what he's doing; he's only acting on instructions from his bosses. But that doesn't alter the facts, does it? He's dangerous. And I'm taking no chances, baby."

Her face became gradually whiter. *Fourteen years*! she thought; I'd rather *die*. She was shaking; he held her to him tightly. Her whisper had the small desolate sound of dead leaves scurrying across concrete: "I knew we'd never get away with it. I knew it from the first."

"It's all right, you little silly. Don't lose your nerve. It's going to be all right."

"It'll never be all right, Rex. We've turned our world into a beastly place, full of deceit and mistrust."

"Oh, come off it, Poll!" he laughed. "All this carry-on because a young man casts sheep's eyes at you! And because for once he's not as genuine as all the others you think the world has come to an end. Why don't you find out for yourself what it is he's really up to. Then you'll know the truth."

She gazed at him steadily for a long silent moment. And then she said:

"All right. I will. Give me the chance, and I will. Tomorrow."

3

When they came downstairs after breakfast the next morning, it was to find that Stephen had already gone out. The day clerk at the reception desk said he had taken his car.

"No message?"

"No message, sir."

"I wonder," Rex mused aloud, as he and Paula traversed the Ramistrasse, "I wonder why he went off by himself?"

"Why don't we leave now while he's away," Paula said in a low voice.

"Because he may be expecting us to do just that. And before I make a move I want to be sure how much he knows. We'll take him dancing tonight. I'll book a table at the Club Terasse."

That same evening, three quarters of an hour after Rex saw Stephen's green Volkswagen return, he mounted to the fourth floor and knocked on the door of Room 485.

"Who is it?"

"Steve! It's me – Ross."

"Just a minute." Rex heard him moving about, and then he opened the door. "Come in."

He stayed just over the threshold, keeping the door ajar, as if he intended to stay but a moment or was not quite certain of his welcome.

"Well what happened to you today?" he said cheerfully. "Sailing off into the blue without a word."

Stephen looked at him with a small smile.

"You don't want me always hanging round your neck," he said lightly, picking a tie off the rail.

"Oh, what rot, my dear fellow." He cast him an affectionate ironical glance. "Here, tell me what you think of this," he said, lobbing; a small package at him.

"What is it?"

"Open it and see."

Rex leaned against the edge of the door, watching him, with his hands behind his back, feeling for the catch on the lock. He slipped it back. "Do you like it?" he said.

"It's a beauty," Stephen said, half-embarrassed by the handsomeness of the gift. "I don't know what to say. It's far better than mine."

"Paula chose it," Rex said carelessly.

"Did she?" said the young man, turning his face away. "It's very nice of you both."

"My dear chap," Rex protested, "it was the least I could do, after chucking yours into the Rhine... c'mon, let's go catch a drink before dinner."

He tapped on Paula's door as they passed on their way down.

"You ready, sweetie?"

"Nearly," she sang out.

"How much longer are you going to be?"

"Ten minutes."

"That means a good half-hour," he assured Stephen knowledgeably, making a comically resigned face.

He was allowing her a clear half-hour for the task. It shouldn't take her that long to find the evidence if it was there. It was only a matter of searching through Stephen's things for some note, some comment, some instruction committed to paper, while he kept Stephen out of the way.

The mistake Rex made was in chumming up with two other Englishmen in the bar, thinking it would make his side of it easier, would make the time appear to pass more rapidly till Paula joined them. In fact, it ruined the careful plan. For after his second Martini, Stephen left them with a murmured excuse, and Rex was obliged to remain chatting affably with the other two, wondering, as the moments passed and Stephen did not return, where the hell he had got to.

*

There was little enough in the way of papers for Paula to go through: a Genevan hotel bill... a leaflet from a bottle of sunburn lotion... half a dozen postcards from the Basle museum... a letter from somebody called Marjorie, beginning "Dear Bro"... a folder of snapshots... a small pocket diary...

She was leafing back through the diary, looking for the date when he had encountered her in Geneva, when a sound outside the door arrested her. She caught her breath, listening to the faint chink of metal. She dropped the diary into the open drawer and softly pushed it to. The heavy metal tab clanked as the key was inserted in the door and turned. There was nowhere she could go; she was trapped. She stood there, frozen, watching the door in a terror of suspense.

Stephen was well inside before he perceived her standing against the chest of drawers on the right-hand wall. He stared, speechless with amazement. The door closed behind him. Tensely across the room her wide regard met his. It seemed that neither of them knew what to say. They might have forgotten how to speak, how to move, so long they stood fixedly staring at one another in silence.

She wondered whether he could hear the beating of her heart. One thought came out of the whirling confusion, now she would know the truth, from his reaction. If he was innocent it would never occur to him in a million years why she was there in his room. But if he instinctively jumped to the conclusion that she had come to look for something, that could only mean he suspected Rex Buchanan's death all this while to be a fraud. She said nothing. She waited to see if he would betray his knowledge.

He broke the silence at last to say in a queer parched voice:

"What are you doing here?"

She made no answer, only kept her eyes on his. Her gaze moved to his mouth. She passed her tongue across her lips:

"What do you think?"

He stared, half-incredulous of her meaning.

"I was waiting for you," she said.

He uttered her name hoarsely.

She said with a suggestion of reproach:

"Why did you keep away from me all day?"

"Oh, God! ..." he cried, and took her in his arms, bruising her mouth with his between muttered endearments.

They parted, trembling, fingers entwined, regarding each other with unsmiling intensity.

"Paula, oh, Paula! ...How did you know I would come up here now?"

"I didn't."

"What made you come?"

"Isn't it enough that I'm here," she murmured, withdrawing her hand from his to unscrew her earring…

*

"Oh, God, I love you so much… so much," he groaned, as they clasped each other in the dark. And at that precise moment came a sound louder than the knocking of their hearts, more insistent than their pounding blood, a quiet muffled tap… tap, tap, tap… she stiffened in his embrace; for the second time in less than a quarter of an hour a wave of panic swept over her. He could feel her body shaking beneath his.

"It's all right," he whispered, as they heard the handle gently creak in its socket, "it's locked, darling, the door's locked." She crammed her knuckles against her mouth, listening to the silence, imagining faint indefinable noises.

"Let me go, Steve, let me go."

"Darling, it's all right. She's gone now. It was only the chambermaid come to turn down the covers, or something."

"It was Rex. I must go, Steve."

"Rex?"

"I mean, Ross. It was Ross."

"Dearest love, why on earth should Ross come here? It was the maid."

She could not tell him why she knew it must be Rex.

"Besides, Ross would have called out if he thought I was here," he argued, holding her wrist as she slipped away from him.

"With the door locked on the inside and the room in darkness? He's not a fool," she said, shivering on the edge of the bed as she stepped into her stilted slippers and drew the folds of her dress over her head. "For that matter, even if it was the maid, she would know why the door was locked."

"Oh, why did it have to be like this," he muttered in despair.

"Turn up the light, Steve."

"You're not angry with me, are you?" he said, watching her run his comb through her hair.

She turned to look at him. She reached out and put her hand behind his head.

"Of course I'm not angry," she said, kissing his eyes.

"And you don't regret?"

"I don't regret."

"'To regret nothing is the beginning of wisdom'."

"So they say," she smiled.

"I loved you even then, the first time I saw you. You know that whatever happens I shall always love you."

"I know."

"More than life itself."

"Please don't, darling. Will you do something for me?"

"Anything in the world."

"Will you go downstairs now and find Ross. Make some excuse for your absence, but don't let him know you've been in your room. I'll join you in a few minutes."

"All right." But still he gazed at her and made no move. "Just tell me before I go…"

"Tell you what?"

"That you love me too."

She turned her face from him with a crooked smile: "Oddly enough, I do."

"Oh darling," he cried, in pain, "what is going to become of us?"

But that was something even Paula could not answer.

*

"Well, where the devil did you get to?" Rex inquired, as Stephen dropped on the bar stool beside him.

"Sorry I had to leave you so long. I had to make a phone call."

"She must be very fascinating, judging by the time it took you," Rex grinned.

Stephen shot him a quick look.

"Not on your life," he laughed, a touch excessively. "It was business, Rex, it always takes an age to get through to London." He didn't notice the slip, but Rex did. "Paula not down yet?" he added idly.

"When you're married to a beautiful woman you have to learn to be patient, my dear Steve."

And a moment later, Paula sailed towards them, cool and imperturbable.

*

"Dirty beasts," said Inge, the chambermaid, primly as she straightened the crumpled bedcovers in Room 485. "Filthy foreigners… atheists… her hand, sliding the under-sheet smooth, encountered a small hard object

124

beneath the pillow. She drew it out. It was an earring, a green earring, too showy and large to be of any value. "I wouldn't wear such muck," she said, holding it by its winking rhinestone stud to the edge of her cheek and contemplating her reflection in the long mirror. The effect was pretty. She found its pair caught in the fringe of the counterpane. "If I wasn't an honest girl," she said, looking at them in her coarse red hand. "It isn't as if they're worth anything..." She laid them neatly together in the center of the table: "There gentleman, keep them as a souvenir. And I hope I didn't spoil your fun."

*

"It's all right, darling, isn't it?" Stephen murmured in her ear on the dance floor of the Club Terasse.

"Yes," she said. "It's all right."

"I told you it would be... I'll see you tomorrow, won't I?"

She smiled.

"I expect so."

When they returned to their table, Rex began to outline a plan for an expedition next day up in the mountains.

"You don't expect me to walk, I hope," said Paula.

"We'll buy you a pair of walking shoes in the morning, darling. And if the worst comes to the worst, I'll pull and Steve can push."

"You do make it sound attractive, like promenading a baby elephant."

"Or a mule."

"Thank you, dear."

"Don't mention it. Come and dance."

She thought, as he swooped across the floor with her: Any minute now, he's going to ask me what happened. But he didn't. He said:

"Just before you joined us in the bar, Stephen made a very curious remark." He spun her round. "I don't know whether it was just a slip, or whether he said it deliberately, watching to see if I would react." He side-stepped and cornered.

"What did he say?"

He held her away, looking down at her with a peculiar expression, and then swung her close again.

"He called me Rex."

If he had looked at her then, he would have seen her face tighten and her eyes grow wide with fear; but she refrained from comment.

"So that, my darling wife, I venture to think just about proves it."

They did not, after all, stay long at the Club Terasse. Paula said she had a headache. They all three went back to the hotel, and Rex's last words as they separated in the lobby were to remind Stephen of their engagement next day.

*

Stephen saw them directly he started to empty his pockets. They glowed up at him with a deep vivid fire, like a dog's eyes in the dark: two perfect cabuchon emeralds, hanging from a single-stone diamond drop. He stared at them stupidly. It took him some moments to grasp how they came to be lying on his bedroom table. It seemed scarcely credible that he should not have noticed her wearing such exquisite objects, though he recalled with perfect clarity the gesture full of significance with which she had put up her hand to remove one of them. He held them up delicately between thumb and finger. His professional experience told him they must be worth, oh, some vast sum, probably two thousand pounds at least. And this one simple fact brought home to him as nothing else had the vast separation this made between them. He had not realized till then how immensely wealthy her husband must be. He placed the earrings in his wallet. Tomorrow, he must make an opportunity to get them back to her discreetly.

His restless sleep was troubled by dreams. He awoke with that clouded, vaguely uneasy, premonition of ill-omen that certain unremembered dreams have the power to cast over the coming day. Feeling heavy-headed and filled with a painful longing to see Paula again, he went downstairs early.

He handed his room-key to the clerk at the reception desk and asked if there was any mail for him. And as the clerk turned to look, he added casually:

"Mr and Mrs Vanbrugh not down yet, I suppose?"

"Yes, sir. They've just left."

"Left! You mean they've gone out."

"No, sir. Mr and Mrs Vanbrugh have checked out with their luggage; we are not expecting them back."

Stephen clung to the desk. He stared at the clerk, shaking his head incredulously from side to side. Checked out, with their luggage! It wasn't possible. Why, they had arranged a picnic in the mountains for today, and the very last thing Ross had said last night… what could have happened to change their minds so suddenly?

"Didn't they leave any message?" he asked dimly.

The clerk pretended to glance at his pad.

"I'm afraid not, Mr Maddox."

He walked away, feeling more piercingly wretched than he had felt since his first term at school; knowing it was over and he would never see her again. She hadn't cared, after all, or how could she have gone without a word!

Could Ross have found out somehow? Perhaps Paula had missed the earrings when she came to undress and…

His hand was on the glass double-doors leading to the restaurant when he thought: *My God, the earrings*! …He was overwhelmed with horror. How was he to get them back to her? He hadn't the remotest notion in die world where she lived, and somehow he *had* to find her. He was in a truly ghastly predicament; he had in his possession a piece of jewelery worth perhaps two thousand pounds, which did not belong to him and its rightful owner had disappeared. To realize that it was almost certainly fully insured came as no solace to an insurance agent, it only increased his sense of responsibility.

He rushed back to the desk.

"Do you know where they've gone?"

"I'm sorry, sir, I don't."

"But they must have left a forwarding address for letters."

"No, sir."

"But that's fantastic. How is one to find them? I've got to get in touch with them; it's terribly important."

"I'm so sorry, Mr Maddox," said the clerk politely.

"There must be some way… their bank? …No, that won't do …they must have filled in a Questionnaire de Séjour, their address would be on that."

"That is for the law, sir. We pass those on to the police authorities."

Glancing about him with feverish helplessness, the glint of gilt lettering caught Stephen's eye. He grabbed hold of the Visitors' Book and leafed through the pages. The confident blue scrawl jumped out at him – Mr and Mrs Ross Vanbrugh. And beside it, the simple legend: England.

It was almost as if they had deliberately cut away all traces. What was he to do? In God's name, what was he to do?

The clerk said:

"If the matter is urgent, Mr Maddox, you could drive out to Kloten Airport and you might catch them before their departure."

"I can try," he said, racing down the hotel steps for his car...

4

It was one of those cold summer mornings when the air is chill with thick early mist. The mountains were shrouded to their shoulders. Visibility at Kloten was too poor for flight: arrivals and departures were temporarily canceled.

Later, it would clear. But later was too late for Rex. He intensely disliked the notion of lingering so near Zurich. He had a fidgety urge to be on the move, to put a league of mountains between himself and Stephen Maddox. He was counting on two or three hours' clear start, for with any luck Maddox would not discover they had gone till half past ten or eleven. That did not mean it would be safe to hang around at Kloten till then. It would make it too easy for Maddox to pick up their trail. The whole point of their sudden and unexplained flight was to escape from Maddox, who had pursued them with such guile, but had at last given himself away by accidentally revealing that he knew Rex's real name, and also by his careless admission (was it purely careless?) that he had put through a call to London. To whom would an unmarried unaffianced man make an expensive trans-continental call? It could only have been to pass an important piece of information or to receive some urgent instruction.

Paula had her own excellent reasons for agreeing with Rex's sudden decision to leave. It would no longer be safe to contend that Stephen was merely an innocent harmless tourist, who liked their company because he was lonely. The whole set-up had become too complicated for her to handle. She could not explain to Rex how Stephen had come to call him that. Easier, wiser, safer to run away. Sometimes, it is the only thing to do.

Rex said:

"If we drive down to Geneva, we can pick up our visas and get a plane from there."

"We might just as well."

"Better than hanging about here, biting our nails."

And thus, Rex was driving back from Kloten as Stephen drove towards it. And on the outskirts of Zurich, where Suchegg Platz crossed Schafthauser Strasse, the green Volkswagen drew up behind two other cars waiting for a pause in the transverse traffic; and as Stephen sat there impatiently tapping his foot, engine pulsing, he saw on the other side of the crossroads the cream-colored Jaguar sweep smoothly down and turn right to join the westward-bound stream of cars... placed as he was behind two other cars, they could not see the Volkswagen as they flashed past. And if he had arrived five seconds later, he would never have seen them. They would have been lost to him for ever.

As it was, they were well ahead, and more than once, he feared he had lost them altogether. It was not so bad as long as they kept to the main roads where there was plenty of traffic and narrow village streets to slow them down from time to time, but it was hard for the Volkswagen to keep up with them on a long open stretch, and impossible to overtake the Jaguar.

It was when they were going up the Lindenberg, and were on the eighth lacée, nearly at the top, that Paula chanced to look down into the dark ravine and observed the little green beetle on the white road far below. Half an hour later, on a straight empty road behind Lucerne, she noticed in the nearside mirror a small green spot a long way behind, and a vague, a still undefinable, apprehension entered her mind.

The third time she saw it it was close enough to be perceived as a Volkswagen. She drew Rex's attention to it.

"By God, if it is...! Do you know his licence number? No, of course you don't. Neither do I. His can't be the only green Volkswagen in these parts. All the same, I'm going to shake him off," he muttered, pushing down on the accelerator. They shot away. But ten minutes later, they were held up at a level-crossing, and by the time the gates opened, the green Volkswagen was at the tail of the line...

In her own way, Paula was every bit as perturbed as Rex. She could not imagine what reckless stupidity had brought Stephen in pursuit of them.

It is hard to realize that it is as easy to mislay a valuable piece of jewelery as a cheap trinket and not be aware of one's loss. In Paula's case, too much had happened too fast the previous evening.

Rex had not been in the room when she fastened on the emerald earrings, or he might well have noticed their absence later. The rapid succession of shocks – being caught by Stephen in his room, the heart-beating seduction, the fright occasioned by that gentle tap at the door interrupting their love-making – all this had wiped the recollection of the earrings from her mind. And afterwards, Rex had rushed her into packing for an early start next day. She had not had a moment to herself in which to straighten out the confusion of her thoughts. And even now, as she sat beside her husband with the jewel case on her knee, nothing in her troubled imagination brought the earrings back to remembrance. Her dread was that for some crazy personal reason Stephen was following them to make a scene. She did not believe he was that kind of senseless fool, she had thought him a quiet and dependable sort of person, but a man in love will sometimes commit imprudences that are quite out of character. The thought created quite a panic inside her. Rex could not drive fast enough to appease her fear.

With masterly ingenuity, Rex twisted back and forth, turning on his tracks, racing up and down the precipitous mountain roads, in the effort to shake off the pursuer. But somehow the little green car always managed to reappear, following them as inexorably as the shadow of some ancient sin.

"It's no good," Rex said, his face grim. "We'll have to try something else. Geneva's out of the question now. I'm going to cross over into France. If he hasn't got his passport on him he'll have to turn back. It's our only chance. Light me a cigarette, Poll… we'll go through Montreux and pick up some food to eat on the other side, I'm getting peckish."

In the distance, across Lake Geneva, the sugar-frosted peaks of Haute Savoie glistened against a poster-blue sky.

What would they do if Stephen got through the Customs and pursued them into France, Paula wondered uneasily. Had Rex thought of that, she wondered, but did not ask. Perhaps she was too afraid.

But Rex had thought of that. He had had plenty of time for thinking on that long hard drive since early morning. Plenty of time to work out a plan in his head. Before they reached Montreux, he had made up his mind.

Up to a point, he had been candid when he told Paula he was crossing into France in the hope that Maddox would not be able to follow, but he kept from her the subtler intention that lay behind it, which was to lure Maddox off Swiss territory and over the border. They had reached the point Paula had foreseen: he had ceased to trust her. Each was now concealing knowledge from the other. The rot had set in.

*

While the French Douane made a perfunctory examination of car and baggage, Rex strolled casually back up the road to the Swiss post to watch for Stephen's car. There was no sign of it. His relief was accompanied by a strange sinking feeling of dismay.

They drove away. Paula closed her eyes thankfully. Only as her muscles slowly relaxed did she realize how tense with strain she had been all this while. She opened her eyes suddenly.

"Why are you driving so slowly?"

"To give him a chance to catch up with us, if he's still following."

She sat up straighter.

"Isn't that rather stupid?"

He gave her an equable glance.

"No. Why? He can't go on chasing us forever, you know. Sooner or later we'll have to face him. Hadn't you realized that?"

"I thought the whole point was that we were trying to get away from him."

"So we were, my dear, so we were. But if we haven't managed it by now we'll have to change our tactics, see. If he has driven two hundred miles and even follows us across the frontier it can only be because he's bloody well determined not to lose us. I want to know why. I want to know just how much he knows. And this is the moment to find out," he added, as the green Volkswagen appeared behind them on the crest of the hill.

"No!" Paula said sharply. "Don't do it, Rex. Please."

But it was no use. It was never any use arguing with Rex, and besides it was too late. With a prolonged fanfare, Rex was already slowing down. He jumped out and ran back to meet the Volkswagen.

"Steve, my dear fellow!" He thrust his head in at the window with a broad smile. "How the devil did you get here?"

Stephen took out a handkerchief and mopped his face.

"God, I'm hot! Talk about follow-my-leader! I wondered where the hell you were taking me. I thought we were supposed to be going to Töss today." It wasn't very good, but it was the best he could do. He had put

132

himself in an absurd predicament, for which there was no valid explanation.

Rex looked at him in amazement.

"You don't mean to say… but didn't you get our message?"

"No."

"We left a message to say we'd been called away. Paula had a wire to say an aunt of hers is dying in Nice."

"I'm sorry."

"Oh, the old girl's had her innings. She's incredibly ancient. But Paula felt she ought to be there. She'll probably perk up when she sees us and take on another lease of life, she's done it before." He added, frowning: "But I say, this is a bad show, isn't it, dragging you all this way?"

"It wasn't your fault. Serves me right for being such an ass, following blindly on, thinking it was some sort of game." He combed his fingers through his ruffled hair. He pressed down the door handle. "Now that I'm here, I'll just say goodbye to Paula," he said, thinking if he ran ahead of Ross down the road he might just have time to push the earrings into Paula's hand with a hurried word of-explanation…

"Nonsense," said Rex easily. "Do you think we're going to let you say goodbye and drive off like that, after coming all this way? Not on your life, laddie. We were just looking out for a nice spot to have a picnic. A crust of bread, a jug of wine, and thou, dear boy, to share it with us. What could be more opportune! Paula will be so pleased." With a wave of the hand he walked back to the Jaguar and climbed in.

"He's joining us for a picnic," he said briefly, letting in the clutch.

"What did he say? Did he tell you why he was following us?"

Rex shrugged.

"He pretends he thought it was some sort of game to do with the outing we had arranged," he said with a sardonic smile. "I could think up a better one than that with my left hand tied behind me. He sadly underestimates my intelligence."

"I wish I knew what was in your mind," Paula muttered. "I can't see the point of all this."

"You will. Leave it to me."

"I wish…" she sighed, and fell silent.

"This looks a good place," he remarked presently, turning the car through a gap in the trees and riding bumpily up the path for twenty yards or so to a small glade richly carpeted with moss and last year's leaves in papery brown curls. "This do you?" he called out as the Volkswagen lurched up behind them.

Stephen slowly descended and stretched himself, gazing up at the pattern of branches interlacing high overhead. "Pretty," he murmured absently. He caught Paula's eye as she lifted the basket of food from the back of the car, and gave her a strange little uncertain smile. "I was so sorry to hear about your aunt," he said, going towards her.

"My aunt?" Paula began, but Rex broke in quickly in his easy manner:

"Those idiots at the hotel never gave the poor chap our message telling him we'd been called away. It's too bad."

"Poor Stephen, what a shame! You must have thought us frightfully rude."

"I wouldn't say that. It's given me the chance to see you both again and say goodbye properly and thank you for everything."

"What rot you do talk, my dear boy, there's nothing to thank us for, the pleasure has all been ours. Hasn't it, Poll? This wine is well and truly *clambré*, almost bath temperature, I'd say. I hope you like your claret hot."

"As long as it's liquid it'll do me fine. I feel as if I've spent the morning inside a vacuum cleaner, hot, noisy and whirling with dust." He raised the plastic beaker in salute: "To – the future. I hope this isn't going to be the end."

"The end of what, my dear fellow?"

"Our friendship. I mean, I hope we're not going to altogether lose touch."

"Listen to him! Of course we're not going to lose touch."

"You'll be returning to England, I suppose, after…?"

"We'll look you up when we do, don't worry, old boy," Rex assured him glibly, chuckling across a *pâté* roll.

"Thanks. But do you know," he gave an unconvincing laugh, "you've never told me where you live."

"We have no home, we are wanderers on the face of the earth, ha ha. But you can always reach us through our bank." He scribbled something on a piece of paper. "There." He held it out, smiling. "You'll be going back to England soon yourself now."

"I'm afraid so," Stephen said with a little grimace. "I wish I didn't have to. It's meant so much to me knowing you – both. More than I can ever tell you." He gazed down at his shoe caps and added in a constrained manner: "I shall never forget it."

"Why, the hypocritical little swine," Rex thought, smiling at him benevolently.

"It's meant a lot to us too, believe me." He stood up, patting back a yawn. "I shall now leave you two to entertain one another while I take a short walk, and then we must proceed on our way, so you might start gathering up the fragments, Poll."

Stephen twisted round, watching him stride purposefully away until he vanished among the dark assembled trees. He expelled a great sigh of relief, turning to face her.

"God! I thought I was never going to get you alone. I've been frantic. I went nearly out of my mind when I found you'd gone. Darling, do you realize—"

"Stephen, you shouldn't have come," she broke in desperately. "It was a dreadfully stupid thing to do."

"I had to come. Paula darling, you don't understand—"

"Oh, we've made such a mess of things between us. If only I could explain…"

"Listen, please listen, darling. I've got to talk to you. It's terribly important. Last night—"

"I know, I know. But please, you must be sensible, Stephen dear. We can't talk about that now, there isn't time. I want you to go now, at once, before he comes back. Don't ask questions, don't argue, just be a dear and go," she implored urgently, inching back, her heels crunching through the fallen leaves, digging into the moss beneath.

He loosed her wrist, shaking his head from side to side in helpless frustration.

"If you'd only *listen* to me for half a minute… I haven't come here to badger you and make a scene. I followed you because I didn't know what else to do. There was no other means of getting in touch with you; I didn't know where you'd *gone*, don't you understand? My only hope was to try and catch up with you and then make some kind of opportunity to get you alone so that I could return them." He spoke with bent head, searching his jacket.

"Return what, Steve? What are you talking about?"

"The earrings," he muttered, his fingers groping in an inner pocket. "I nearly died of fright when I found them on my dressing-table, I was so afraid you'd—"

He had them in his hand, had half risen to his knees to pass them across to her, when he saw her face bleach into pure terror, a frozen, open-mouthed mask of horror carved for some ancient Greek tragedy.

He had time for the thought to pass through his mind that she was exaggerating the calamity with quite ludicrous extravagance; a potential disaster had ended well, nothing was going to happen—

But before he could finish the thought, the world exploded inside his skull. The noise shattered him like an annihilating blow. Or perhaps it was the violence of the blow that produced the effect of noise. He could not tell. There was no time. Time had come to an end.

His hands tightened convulsively on the earrings in his grasp, and he toppled slowly forward in a mockery of oriental obeisance till his forehead touched the earth, politely exposing to Paula's gaze the small wicked hole in the back of his head where her husband had shot him from behind.

5

A startled clapping of wings whirring up from the trees accompanied the echo reverberating through the wood. Paula screamed, released at last – too late – from her paralyzing fear at the sight of the gun muzzle, like a round unwinking black eye, staring at her steadily from the bush. Her scream rang out in the tremulous silence, shocking her own ears: she put a shaking hand over her mouth and slithered backwards, scrabbling in the dead leaves, her appalled gaze clinging to the terrifying object at her feet. The body had fallen sideways, subsiding with its face on the ground. A bead of dark blood trickled from the edge of the wound and was trapped in the thick brown hair.

Perhaps five seconds had passed since he fired the shot – to Rex a time as immeasurable as a fainting spell. He had not moved. His limbs trembled as if from some violent exertion. This peculiar reaction confused him. His mind felt numbed. He could not understand it. He kept trying to explain to himself that this wasn't the first man he had killed, not by a long chalk. During the war... was killing not murder when it was sanctioned by public opinion? Or was it only murder when you could see your victim? Why should it be worse to kill a man at ten feet than to kill twenty persons from two thousand feet? It was nonsense. Nerves. Nothing was altered. The sun still shone blandly down from the immaculate blue.

And yet now the rays that pierced through branch and leaf seemed sharp as blades, stabbing down in relentless accusation at the crime they revealed. Nothing was altered; yet everything was changed.

To his disturbed fancy, the slim tree-trunks surrounding him had become dark, innumerable, barring his way, hemming him in. He was visited by the uncomfortable sensation of being watched on all sides by countless unseen eyes.

The universe itself had become antagonistic, inimical. The ancient moral law rolled through his mind like distant thunder: murdered blood does cry out from the ground. It cries out, and the universe hears; hears, and responds.

Nothing is altered: but everything is changed.

He forced himself to dismiss these unbalancing fancies from his mind. He forced his brain to obey his will. In an orderly fashion, he set about tidying up the disorder his will had imposed. (He knew exactly what had to be done: every detail had been worked out in advance).

So little time had passed that the barrel of the revolver was still hot as he slipped it into his pocket and knelt down beside the dead man. A faint eerie humming caught his attention. He glanced up.

Hunched on her knees facing him, Paula was moaning softly into the hand pressed against her mouth, as she rocked back and forth. She looked drawn, pinched, ugly.

It flashed across his mind: "So that's what she'll look like when she's old," and was repulsed by the thought.

"Oh God, what have you done! …Oh, my God, what have you done! …What have you done! What have you done!" she moaned. Her staring eyes accused him of a deed for which there could be no pardon.

He said:

"I had to do it. There was no other way."

She said, aghast, as though the full horror had only just penetrated her brain:

"*You killed him!*"

As if he were explaining a reasonable fact to a child, he said:

"I had to. There was no other way."

Phrases formed in her mind and sank away unfinished, never to be uttered. She wanted to tell him that he was mistaken, that Stephen had known nothing… but her own guilt barred the way. She could not disavow her own complicity in his death. Between them they had betrayed an innocent man. If she had spoken earlier… now there was nothing that could be said. It was too late. He was dead. Rex had shot him. From behind.

The fact was more nauseating than the mind could bear. An unendurable thought produces its own physical reaction: the body moves, walks, runs, in an attempt to escape from it. Paula climbed stiffly to her feet and fumbled her way blindly from tree to tree. She had no idea where she was going, she moved only to get away from her thoughts. She did not think; that is, her thoughts did not make an orderly coherent sequence, but flashed irrelevantly here and there like small silvery fish darting erratically through water, swerving ever and again in fright from the stony boulders of reality blocking the way. "Let it be all right! …Make it never have happened! …" a trapped terrified creature inside her cried dumbly in the wordless abject prayer that has no destination.

Rex went quickly through the dead man's pockets and removed papers, wallet, passport, keys, monogrammed handkerchief – everything that might lead to his identification if the body ever was found. (He could not know that he had left behind the one vitally important object, the cause of Stephen Maddox's death, still clutched in the dead hand…) He dragged the body into the shelter of a clump of bushes, concealing it beneath the low-spread boughs, kicking up the leaves to cover the limbs. It might be years before the body was discovered in a place like this – a few acres of woodland on the edge of nowhere. The car was a different matter to dispose of.

He came upon Paula leaning against a tree, her face against the rough bark.

"Are you all right?" he said. He touched her shoulder. She turned her head to look at him without speaking. "Are you all right?" he said again. "Paula, we have to get away from here." She shook her head, as though she did not comprehend. "Come on, you must pull yourself together," he urged, and again laid a hand on her arm. She gazed down at his hand and suddenly she began to tremble.

"Ohhh, why did you do it?" she muttered in a parched voice and her eyes filled with tears, which spilled out, faster and faster, to fall in burning drops on to his hand – the atrocious murderer's hand, on whose tender strength she had for so long relied. The hateful present rendered all the past intolerable. Her stomach revolted, as if to heave out past and present together in one fierce spasm of rejection.

"She's upset, it's only natural," he thought. "It was a shock to her. Women haven't the stamina of men. I didn't like it much myself. I'm not a murderer, after all. But it had to be done, if we were ever to sleep peacefully for the rest of our lives. Women don't understand expediency."

She was ice-cold now and shivering.

"Poor darling," he said. "There's some wine in the car. You'll be better when you have a drink inside you." And he began to urge her gently in that direction (he was desperate to get away).

"I'm all right," she said sharply. "Let me alone. Don't touch me."

"All right." He made a gesture of letting her pass.

She glanced round at the empty space where lately she had been sitting, and made her decision.

"Where's my handbag?"

"In the car."

She went over and picked it up.

"Ready?" he said, holding open the door. "You'll have to drive. I'm taking the Volkswagen."

She looked at him steadily and shook her head.

"No," she said. She was stone cold and shaking with fear, but she had made her decision. "I'm not going with you."

"Oh, God," he thought, wearily, "she's going to make a scene."

"Look, Poll, do get in," he said reasonably. "Let's for God's sake get *away*! We can't argue here."

"I'm not going with you," she repeated, and began to walk away, stumbling a little in the thick leaves covering the uneven ground.

He caught hold of her.

"And where do you think you're going, may one ask?"

"I don't know. I only know I'm leaving you. I can't stay with you any longer."

"If it were as simple as that, I'd let you go. But it can't be done, my dear. We're in a situation that we can't run out of, either of us. Do you understand?"

"You can't make me stay if I want to leave. It's no good bullying and threatening. Let go of my arm, please. Let go of me," she said, her voice rising as she struggled to wrench herself free.

"I'm not threatening you, any more than I'm *asking* you to stay: I'm *telling* you."

"Take your hands off me!" she shrieked, hating him, hating the touch of his hands.

This was hysteria. He hit her twice, hard, across the face. She staggered and fell in an awkward heap on the ground.

"Have I made myself clear now?" he said, pulling her to her feet.

She gasped with shock, her hand to her cheek, and broke into painful weeping.

"Now get in," he said, pushing her into the driver's seat. "You're going to help me finish this, whether you like it or not. I'm going to drive his car, and you will follow, till I've disposed of it. When that's done, you'll pick me up. You understand? There's nothing difficult or dangerous about it. You have only to keep right behind me so that no other car can cut in between us. Have you got that? And don't try anything stupid. Are you ready?"

"I can't," she whispered, tears sliding down her face. "I can't do it."

"Start the engine," he said. "Go on. Start the engine."

She stretched out her hand and switched on the ignition. The motor began to throb. She heard him move away, the leaves crunching under his feet. She sat there, thinking of nothing, feeling nothing but a great exhaustion, a weary capitulation, gushets of tears springing freshly from her eyes each time she wiped them away.

The Volkswagen backed and turned, and lurched slowly towards the road...

He turned the car back into the mountains. He recollected passing some ten miles away a stretch of road so narrow and precipitous that it appeared to curve into space. It dropped sheerly away to a narrow gorge two thousand feet below. A stone Cross had been erected at the roadside in memory of the many people who had driven to their death at that spot.

He drove towards it steadily, keeping an eye on the Jaguar in the mirror. The sun vanished behind the peaks. The steep, rock-ribbed walls grew darker, more menacing, pressing closer. There was no difference between one piece of road and the next now, it was just a white track cut in the black rock, winding on and on, round bend after bend. He began to be afraid of missing the place. Perhaps he had passed it already. Light had fled from the valley below, leaving it in navy shadow with a curling white feather of water glinting at the bottom.

He came upon it suddenly. The stone Cross stood out clearly, backed by the darkness of the mountain opposite. He signaled to the Jaguar, slowed down, drove carefully to within a few inches of the edge, put it into reverse, and braked, leaving the engine running. He slid across and jumped out. He stood at the roadside, hands in pockets, like any tourist enjoying a spectacular view. (He had first to be sure no car was approaching; it would not do to be observed in the act).

A ten-ton camion swung round the corner, the driver leaning from his cabin to shout furiously at the Volkswagen's imprudent owner, raising his arms in an impassioned gesture. The lorry drove on, and then, just past the Jaguar, ground to a halt. Rex had barely time to sign to the Jaguar to start rolling again, before the driver climbed down and began to run towards him.

"*Vous êtes en panne, m'sieur?*"

The Jaguar slid past.

Rex turned with a vague uncomprehending smile, and shook his head. He waved an admiring hand at the frowning peaks.

"*Alors, quoi! Vous voulez vous suicider, donc?*" the lorry-driver cried irritably. "*C'est idiot ce que vous faites là, vous savez. Pourrait arriver un accident. ACCIDENT!*" he shouted to the foreign fool grinning politely back at him. He threw up his hands in despair and with a shrug turned on his heel.

The lorry spluttered to life and with a savage clash of gears, shot away. The Jaguar had turned the corner and was out of sight. He had a touch of crawling panic at the thought that Paula might not be waiting for him down the road, that she might have seized her chance and gone. He refused to admit the possibility. He didn't believe she would do that, he didn't believe she could. The incident with the lorry-driver was quite bad enough. Quite bad enough that he had been noticed; that he had been seen at such close quarters that the man would be able to recognize him again; that he would remember having stopped to warn him; that he had probably noted the Volkswagen's number. Quite bad enough, and no good worrying about it now, Rex decided, opening the off-side door and leaning in to release the brake …

It rolled slowly back, hung poised a moment with its rear wheels in the air, and went over, crashing down with a formidable din as it fell…

He was running towards the distant Jaguar, before it hit the bottom of the ravine…

6

Darkness came on. He had been driving for some hours.

"We'll stop the night at Dijon," he announced.

She made no comment. She did not even turn her head from its steady gaze at the almost invisible landscape flowing past in the deepening twilight. She had not spoken once since he got into the car. "Move over," he had said, taking her place at the wheel. And she had moved over without a word. After that he had scarcely spoken, apart from a few mumbled remarks about the reckless habits of other drivers, more to himself than to her. He did not seem aware of her silence. Or if he noticed it, it was only to be grateful for it. He wanted to think.

It was about nine o'clock when they drove through the outskirts of Dijon. He stopped before a hotel in a broad lighted square in the center of the town.

"Will this do?"

She didn't answer. But when he got out of the car she followed him into the hotel.

"Have you a room for the night?" he asked the receptionist.

"*Two* rooms," said Paula.

Rex looked at her quickly, but she was gazing straight ahead at the receptionist, who glanced uncertainly from one to the other.

"Monsieur and madame would like a suite?" the receptionist suggested intelligently.

"That isn't necessary," Paula said. "I only want a room to myself."

"The suite will do very well," said Rex. "And can we have something to eat?"

"Certainly, monsieur."

Paula said:

"I don't want anything to eat, thank you, I'm not hungry. I should like to go straight to my room. Would you see that my luggage is brought up to me."

She walked away in the direction of the gilt-wrought lift.

"Paula!" Rex said in a low bewildered voice. She passed him without a glance. His hand dropped futilely to his side. "Madame is tired. It's been a long day," he said heavily without raising his eyes.

Later, when he tried her door, he found it locked. He tapped.

"*Qui est là?*" he heard her call.

"It's me, Paula, please let me in a minute." There was no response. "Poll," he said in a pleading tone, "what's the matter?" He was genuinely disconcerted. Nothing like this had ever occurred between them. Their quarrels had never been of this nature. Paula's present attitude was quite out of character. Silence was not her weapon. Their disagreements were passionate, not cold negation. And however violently they might quarrel they had never slept apart. He gave up at last and went away feeling profoundly uneasy.

"She'll be all right tomorrow," he told himself. "A good night's sleep..." He was desperately tired himself. So tired suddenly that he could hardly undo his buttons. He fell into bed and sank out of consciousness in a deep dreamless slumber.

*

In the service room on the fourth floor of the St Gott-hard Hotel, Inge, the chambermaid, picked up the house-phone and got through to the reception desk.

"Herr Werner? ...Good morning, Herr Werner. Inge Schnell here. Lovely day, isn't it? ...Oh, Herr Werner, ha ha! I'm surprised at you. Nothing of the kind. It's the Englishman in 485. He's not in his room, and his bed's not been slept in... oh, Herr Werner, ha ha! And it wouldn't be the first time either, I can tell you..."

And Herr Werner glancing casually at the pigeon-holes behind him observed that the key to Room 485 dangled from its hook. He continued sorting the morning mail. A minute or two later a waiter passed through the lobby. "Giovannini!"

"Herr Werner."

He beckoned him over.

"Did Mr Maddox, the Englishman at table 29, dine in the restaurant last night?"

"I'll find out."

But it was breakfast time and Giovannini was busy. It was half an hour before he had a moment to get through to Herr Werner with the information he wanted.

"The gentleman wasn't in to any meals yesterday." "What gentleman? What are you talking about?"

"The Englishman, Herr Werner. Table 29."

"Oh, wasn't he? Very good."

Herr Werner rang through to the hotel garage and inquired if Herr Maddox's car was there. It had been out since yesterday morning, they said. Herr Werner made a note of the make and licence number, and sighed. These affairs were always a great nuisance; but duty was duty. He picked up the other telephone and put through a call to the Zurich police.

"Hallo? St Gotthard Hotel here. We wish to notify you that one of our guests has been missing for twenty-four hours... no, he didn't, naturally... English... Stephen Maddox... yes, a green Volkswagen, number GDX 2778: GB..." He doodled idly two eyes and a severely Greek nose. "A road accident, I don't know what else, I'm sure ... I'm delighted to hear it... no, I've no idea... then, if anything's reported, you'll let us know... naturally... any time... at your service." He hung up. Now it was out of his hands.

And at the police station, the radio-telephonist sent out a road-call for information concerning a green Volkswagen from Great Britain, number GDX 2778, possibly involved in a road accident...

*

It was much later than Rex intended when he awoke. He had meant to get away to an early start. But it was gone half past eight when he wakened. His senses were confused, his mind troubled with an obscure feeling of apprehension. "I've slept too heavily," he told himself, thrusting back the bedclothes. He plunged his head into cold water. But the dismal cloud persisted all the while he was dressing and re-packing his toilet necessities. It was absurd for a grown man to be bothered to the point of distress because his wife was quarreling with him, but there lay the root of his unease. It was the first time her judgment had gone against him. And that it should be now, of all times, when he most needed her moral support! He hadn't wanted to kill the wretched man. It had been purely a matter of necessity, like striking down a cobra before it struck you. He hoped to God Paula would see it differently after a night's sleep.

Paula was waiting for him when he came downstairs. She was sitting in the hotel lobby, glancing at a folded English newspaper on the table beside her, one hand resting on the jewel-case in her lap.

He stood over her.

"Did you have a good night?" he said pleasantly.

The brutal stupidity of the remark brought the blood flushing to her face; but she made no reply.

"I'm afraid I overslept," he said. "Have you been waiting long?" She continued to ignore him, and he felt a spasm of rage surging up. He would have liked to shake her as she sat there reading the paper with that air of studied indifference. He bent down.

"Must you be so goddamned ostentatious in your disapproval in front of everyone?" he hissed angrily at her ear.

Her eyes were stony in the glance she turned coldly upon him, but he was pleased to observe the newspaper shook in her grasp.

When he had paid the bill and brought the car round, he went back to her.

"If you're quite ready, let's go," he said in a sullen tone.

*

Gradually, the bright agreeable day soothed him, wrought on him a change of mood. The prospect of being on their way to Central America before the day was over, calmed him, dissipating all his present anxieties and irritations. Everything would seem different once they were there. Distance would render the past as remote as childhood. There would never be any cause for worry again. He filled his mind with visions of handsome white buildings and broad tree-lined streets... a patio screened by palms and exotic with tropical shrubs... Paula laughing with him in the sunshine... and the cool evocative music of ice tinkling in long glasses...

Absorbed in these pleasant reflections he forgot the heavy cloud overhanging the present. Or, rather, it ceased to seem important.

"Old girl," he said affectionately, squeezing her knee.

Paula brushed his hand roughly aside. She said through clenched teeth:

"Just don't touch me. Do you understand?"

"Still sulking?"

146

"I just never want to feel your hands on me again, that's all."

"Why, Poll!" Half shocked, half laughing, totally uncomprehending, he took his attention from the road a moment to look at her. "You talk as if..." The car swerved and he set it straight again. He said: "Why are you so angry?" '

"Angry!" she uttered an incredulous sound akin to a laugh.

"Poll, I'm sorry. I really am," he said with a contrite air and tried to slip his fingers through hers.

She drew sharply away. She sat bolt upright, trembling, pressing down the catch on the door.

"I shall throw myself out if you touch me again. I mean it."

He exclaimed:

"Good God, you're hysterical!"

"You see," she said evenly, "I would rather kill myself than be touched by your murderer's hands."

He jumped at the word, as if it had stabbed on a nerve, it came so unexpectedly. He changed color. He became white, and then silent. He wasn't appalled to think of himself as a murderer, but it appalled him that Paula should see him like that – with conventional horror and loathing. It was as frightening as though part of his own body had rebelled against him.

"If that's how you feel about me," he said after a while, "it doesn't make a very hopeful prospect for the future."

"There can't be any future, can there, for either of us now?"

"Why not?" he said. "Nothing is altered."

"Nothing is altered! We are, Rex. We are altered."

"Oh, don't be so goddamned portentous," he cried suddenly, banging his hands down on the steering-wheel in an excess of irritation. "What did you expect me to do?"

She said quietly:

"I didn't expect you to commit a murder."

"I had no choice," he cried. "You know that."

"You had a choice," she insisted, very low. "And you chose to kill him..." Her voice trembled. "An unsuspecting man..." she added.

"It was to save you from prison, you might remember that while you're being so bloody self-righteous."

"And yourself."

"All right, and myself. I don't deny it. I've no more wish to spend half my remaining years in jail than you have. The only difference is that I admit it and you'd like to pretend that it had nothing to do with you. You want to crawl out of it and leave all the responsibility on me."

"I'm not responsible," she cried. "It had nothing to do with me. I didn't know what you were going to do. My God, I'd rather spend the rest of my life in prison than have the murder of an innocent man on my conscience."

"Would you indeed? What bloody sentimental rot you talk. Do you think I *liked* doing it?"

"You knew what you were going to do, you planned it. And you sat there laughing and joking, *knowing* you were going to shoot him. That's what makes it so terrible. That's what I can't bear to think you could do. He liked you, he looked on you as a friend, poor trusting boy," Paula said bitterly.

"While we're ripping everything apart, let's tear down that bit of fantasy too. It wasn't me he liked and looked on as a – to keep that politely ambiguous designation – friend, was it, my dear? Did you think I was blind? I was perfectly aware of how he felt about you. The poor trusting boy," he said sardonically, "given half a chance wouldn't have hesitated to betray me with my wife. Let's face it: that's what all the fuss is about, isn't it? That's really what you are blaming me for, killing a man who was in love with you." He glanced at her sideways. "And all this sudden hatred for me is really the hatred you feel for yourself, because you knew that at the same time he was doing his best to hunt us down and you couldn't face the issue."

"You are mistaken," she said. "He wasn't in any way involved in that, as it happens."

"No? It was all sheer coincidence, running into you in Geneva, following you to Zurich... and he pursued us all the way to France just to see you again, I suppose."

"If you want to put it like that, yes. It was to see me... and say goodbye. You killed him for nothing." She pressed a handkerchief to her lips. "If you want to know why I hate you, isn't that a good enough reason, that you killed an innocent man?"

"I've killed many innocent men in my time. I've no way of knowing how many. It's considered justifiable in war. You never seemed to mind about them. But, of course, they weren't in love with you. I suppose that makes a difference." He lapsed into silence, considering the matter, and presently added, almost idly: "I wonder how you'd have felt about it if you hadn't been in love with him too."

She didn't answer. And after a moment he looked at her and said:

"You were in love with him, weren't you?"

"Yes," she said at last. "Yes, I was, if you want to know."

"I thought so," he said, stretching his lips in a kind of smile. "I thought there was something behind all this carry-on you've been putting me through. We're getting to the truth at last, aren't we? My God, how deceitful you women are! 'Oh, don't touch me, don't touch me!'" he minced in an angry falsetto, "'I can't have anything more to do with you; you've killed a man, you nasty brute!' Oh God, we're so delicate and nice in our feelings, aren't we? An *innocent* man! By God, an *innocent* man!"

"Shut up!" she cried savagely. "For Christ's sake shut up!"

Rex looked pleased for the first time since they had commenced this bitter argument: he had got her wincing now, and the knowledge was like ointment on his bruised masculine vanity. He lit a cigarette, thinking out fresh malice with which to wound her.

They quarreled all the way to Paris. And were still wrangling as he drove down the Avenue Friedland into the Boulevard Haussmann.

He was making for the Guatemalan Legation in the Rue de Courcelles to get the visas permitting them to enter the country: they could then drive straight out to Orly Airport and arrange their departure. But when he came to where the Rue de Courcelles crossed the broad Boulevard he happened to turn to the right instead of the left. (Such a trivial mistake to have made). He crawled along, peering at the numbers, which became consecutively lower, and realized he was going in the wrong direction.

"Damn," he thought, as he debouched into the Rue de la Boétie, "I shall have to circle back to Haussmann." He swung the car into the Faubourg St Honoré, and drew up behind a long double line of stationary cars stretching as far as the eye could see. They were caught in one of those interminable traffic jams that are the bane of city life. A stream of cars closed up behind them.

"You'd better give me your passport," he said, slouching back in his seat and closing his eyes.

"What for?"

"So that I can get it stamped with your visa for Guatemala. The Legation is only just around the corner."

"No thanks."

"What do you mean?"

"I mean, you needn't bother. I'm not going with you to Guatemala, or anywhere else. Haven't you grasped that yet?"

He sat up straight and gave a spiteful laugh.

"And what exactly do you propose to do?"

"That's no concern of yours."

"Oh, don't be so damned silly," he exclaimed in exacerbation, "do you really imagine I'd let you waltz off on your own, with all there is at stake?"

"I'd be amused to know how you think you can prevent me."

"My God, I'd like to wring your neck, you obstinate bitch!" he said in a tone of hardly-suppressed fury.

"Well, why don't you? A bit too public perhaps. You do better when you can take your victim unawares, don't you?"

"How you do bring that in at every opportunity."

"You see, that will always be how I picture you in my mind now, creeping up to shoot him unseen."

"For God's sake," he said, casting a nervous glance at the man in the car alongside, "keep your voice down, can't you?"

"You didn't give him a chance."

"You think I should have held him up like a movie villain while I told him precisely what I was going to do and why. You've seen too many films, my dear," he was saying with a dry laugh, when to his utter surprise and consternation Paula suddenly sprang out of the car and ran back through the motionless traffic across the road towards the Rue de la Boétie...

"Paula! ...Paula! ..." he called helplessly, craning his head round to watch the running figure, darting among the strollers on the opposite pavement, her handbag under one arm and the jewel case in her other hand banging against her thigh as she ran...

He had perhaps half a minute in which to decide what to do. Soon she would be out of sight, and once that happened all would be lost. He had to stop her. And here he was, wedged in the middle of a traffic jam that seemed as if it would never move again, while she disappeared with their fortune. There was only one thing to do. He left the car where it was and went after her. She would be hampered by her tight skirt, he would soon catch her up.

Paula threw a hurried glance over her shoulder as she turned the corner and was struck with horror to see him striding after her. Her heart thumping, she fled down a side-street…

It is always frightening to be chased. The special circumstances added a nightmare quality to her flight. She ran for her life, instinctively, without conscious thought, not knowing where she was going.

People turned to stare in astonishment at the sight of a well-dressed woman, her slim skirt pulled above her knees, running as if her life depended on it, and passed on with tolerant amused shrugs. But all that Paula saw when she looked behind her was his head bobbing above the other passers-by in her wake. She ran blindly on, diving into every side turning she came to…

The pain in her side was acute agony… she was panting… breathless… the sound of her heart's desperate thudding was like running footsteps in her ears…

She stumbled into the Boulevard Malesherbes. "I can go no further," she thought, hanging on to the iron paling round a tree. A god appeared in a machine beside her – a fat bad-tempered-looking god, but divine! She almost fell into the machine's interior. It was like a reprieve.

"*Vite*," she said faintly. "*Vite!*"

"*Mais où, donc?*" he demanded irascibly, slamming down the flag.

"*N'importe*," she said with a frantic gesture. "Just *go*, can't you?" She snatched a look through the back window, prepared to leap out of the taxi again if the wretched man would waste precious seconds arguing. She was at weeping point. "*On me suit!*" she cried desperately.

"*Ah ha!*" He gave a roguish chuckle. "*C'est comme ça, hein?*" With an air of reckless gallantry, he shot out into the middle of the road…

It was at least a respite, in which to gather herself together and think what was to be done.

The certitude that she must leave Rex had been with her ever since that hour in the wood. It was a passionate decision; ways and means didn't enter into it – she hadn't given a thought to how she would leave him, or when, or what she would do afterwards. All night long her beating heart had said: "You must get away… you must get away…" And on the long journey to Paris, the stubborn conviction within her grew more certain with every word he uttered, as if his words were winding up a piece of clockwork inside her, till it reached the point where the clockwork must be released or snap: and unable to endure another minute of it, she had jumped from the car. It was a blind impulse. Or she would never have taken the jewel case. She just happened to have it in her hand when she jumped out. Just that. She wasn't actually aware even yet, in her distraught state of mind, that she had it with her.

She had recovered her breath and was watching anxiously through the rear window for the Jaguar or a taxi which seemed to hang too persistently behind; she saw no sign of either. Sinking back thankfully, she became aware that she was in a district that was unfamiliar to her. She thought: "Where am I? And where am I going? I can't drive round Paris for ever."

Of course! It was obvious what she must do. She rapped on the glass screen.

"*Allez à la Gave du Nord,*" she requested.

Once she was in England she would be safe. Rex would never follow her there. Besides, he wouldn't know where she had gone. Very likely he had given her up already in his concern to get away to Central America while there was still time.

A wave of pure terror flushed through her body. He couldn't go: she had the jewels! "Oh, God," she thought, "dear God, no wonder he ran after me!" A hundred thousand pounds in this little box. The fortune he had sweated for over three years. He would never let it go, never. What was she to do? She didn't want it, she didn't want to have anything to do with it, God knows she didn't. To carry it around was like a murderer walking the streets with a knife dripping with the blood of his victim. It constituted an unparalleled danger not only to her but to Rex too. Because – who knows – Stephen's body might already have been discovered. And once that happened there would also be found the earrings clutched in the dead hand, revealing an unmistakable connection with the crime. The French police might find it difficult to identify the body, but those costly and valuable gems in their unusual settings would be simple to trace … as distinguishable as a finger-print. And of this danger Rex was totally ignorant, because he didn't know the earrings were missing. She must somehow get rid of this burden. It occurred to her that the best way would be to deposit the case at the Left Luggage office, and then – if she had the courage – destroy the ticket.

The taxi drew up at the station entrance. She got out with a swift glance round and paid him off. The rank smell of soot and urine mingled with the din of trucks thundering over concrete and shunting trains and engine whistles, rising with a hollow sound into the grimy vault. First, she must get a ticket and find out the time of the trains. The board of announcements was between the entry to two platforms. Paula walked over to it, and as she approached, she beheld, waiting by the platform where the trains for Calais departed, the tall figure of her husband… her heart gave a great leap of terror.

"Dear Heaven," she thought, "he knew this was where I'd come; he was expecting me." He knew from long familiarity the way her mind worked. And at that moment he turned his head and saw her. His eyes met hers, holding them in a long frightening stare. Her throat was parched with fear. She had a clear unreasoning conviction that he was going to kill her, now, among these crowds of people. Panic locked her limbs, as in a nightmare, only this was a nightmare from which she couldn't awaken because she was awake already. But as he moved towards her the spell was broken; she whirled round and fled, pushing through the throng of people streaming to their trains.

Her taxi was gone, and there was not another unoccupied one to be seen. She ran across the road, with Rex no more than five yards behind, and jumped on an autobus as it pulled away from the kerb. Rex made a spurt, but it had already gained too much speed, and he began to drop back. Paula saw him raise his arm and, as the bus swung round a corner, she saw a taxi draw up beside him.

Paula was on the overcrowded outside platform, crushed between a massive housewife and a gentleman who was making very French explorations of her person (she wished wryly he would pinch the accursed jewel box instead of herself), watching Rex's cab weaving in and out in their wake. She couldn't think what to do. He would undoubtedly follow the bus until he saw her descend. Even among all these people she could not hope to get out unobserved by him. She would not stand a chance on foot while he had the advantage of a motor. If only the suit she was wearing of palest dove-gray silk didn't make her so dreadfully visible! She touched the pigeon's breast confection of feathers on her head, and had a second's wild impulse to offer it to the large lady beside her in exchange for her black mushroom. But such a proposition was out of the question, naturally. Well, what was she to do? She couldn't stay on the autobus for ever. She didn't even know where it was going.

She bought a *carnet* of tickets from the conductor and tore off six haphazard.

"*Les Galeries Lafayette*," shouted the conductor.

She thought:

"Of course, that's it."

It would be easy to shake him off among all those departments. She could slip out by another door.

She thought:

'He'll have to pay off the taxi, that'll give me a few moments' start. If I wait till the last he won't be expecting me to get off, it'll take him by surprise. I'm going to risk it. It's now or never.'

The conductor struck the bell and Paula leaped down, bolted across the pavement, through the swing-doors... she walked hurriedly past the cosmetics, the stockings, the haberdashery, the handbags – when an idea struck her and she turned back to make a hasty purchase. Displayed among the handbags were several capacious canvas-and-leather zip-fastened overnight bags. She chose the first that came to hand. She had just paid for it and was slipping the jewel box inside, when a sixth sense warned her to look round. Rex was standing in the middle of the floor, looking for her. Without waiting for her change, she moved swiftly away. But it was too late; he had seen her.

There began then a grim and ludicrous game as if they were children playing "tag" among the grown-ups, according to some mysterious rules of their own. Round and round they went, pursuer and pursued dodging up one aisle and down the next, a square of counters always between them, keeping to a quick walking-pace, each obeying the pretence of being normal shoppers – for however desperate the reason, one cannot start running through the departments of a public store.

As they edged round the cosmetics, someone bumped into Rex and an edifice of powder boxes clattered to the ground, spinning hither and thither. In the moment's confusion while he turned to apologize, Paula made a dash for the exit.

In a second he was after her, pounding twenty yards behind her as she sprinted round the first corner she came to, up the Rue Mogador, and then down the Rue Caumartin. A little further along was the Magasin du Printemps. She darted inside and saw across the floor a cluster of people pushing their way into the lift. She sped across and flung herself, panting, through the doors just before they closed. As Rex reached it, it soared away.

He took the stairs three at a time, pausing at each floor to wait for Paula to get out, but the lift rose to the top and smartly descended without disgorging her.

"It was a feint, a trick to give her a chance to double on her tracks," Rex decided indignantly, racing down again. The lift sailed past three floors without stopping. It was now well ahead. And when he reached the ground floor once more, the lift was empty. Paula was gone, vanished. He glared around for her in desperation. She couldn't have had time to get to an exit. She must have contrived to slip out somewhere on the way down.

The lift attendant leaned negligently in the doorway, picking her nails. He went up to her, forcing a smile.

"I've lost my wife," he said in his clumsy French. "She went up with you. I wonder can you tell me which floor she got out at. A svelte lady in pale gray, about your height."

She gave him a languid look of appraisal.

"*Au premier, monsieur*," she said, pointing upwards with the gesture of an admonitory angel in a cemetery.

He mounted to the first floor and wandered uncomfortably among the elegant arrangements of suits and coats and dresses. The atmosphere was hushed, velvety, sacred; he felt as if he was trespassing in the precincts of the Eleusinian Mysteries of the Bona Dea. A saleswoman swam up to him prettily.

"*Monsieur désire?*"

"*Je cherche ma femme,*" he said, raising a hand to shoulder-level to indicate her height and then drawing both hands down a few inches apart to illustrate her slenderness.

"*Mais, asseyez-vous, monsieur,*" the woman said with a charming smile, offering him a chair. "I will go and see."

He could not sit down. He paced restlessly to and fro, terrified that this might turn out to be another ruse of some sort, and yet afraid to go.

*

The sound of his voice reached Paula in the changing-booth, where she was trying on a loose duster-coat of black grosgrain to conceal the pale gray suit; that is to say, she heard a man's voice and knew instinctively that it must be Rex. And suddenly, she was overwhelmed with a feeling of hopelessness. Almost she walked out, there and then, to confront him and as it were give herself up, putting an end to the whole intolerable business. What use to prolong this pointless anguish? Why should she imagine she could escape staying with him to the bitter end? She was simply too weary to fight on. She had arrived at a point beyond fear.

A vague white blur appeared in the dusky depths of the long glass before her. Paula repressed with difficulty a little scream (so much for being beyond fear!) and put a hand to her heart.

The saleswoman began to say – "Ah, pardon, did I startle madame," when madame laid a finger mutely against her lips. The woman stepped close and smoothed the coat over the shoulders with little pats of approval. And as she did so, murmured in the lady's ear: "*Il y a un monsieur là-bas qui vous attend.*"

Paula nodded. She found a scrap of paper in her bag and scribbled on it in French:

'I don't want to see him. Please get rid of him for me. Tell him I've already left.'

In a little while the woman returned with a mischievous smile to say he was gone.

"*Merci bien, mademoiselle.*"

"*Ah, les hommes…*" said the other, casting up her eyes.

Paula paid for the coat and waited for the time it took her to smoke a cigarette, so as to be quite certain the coast was clear. Then she went up to the Ladies' Rest Room on the top floor. Here at least, she was safe. Here was one place he could not follow her, she thought thankfully, sinking into a deep chair.

Ladies were fussing with their persons before the numerous mirrors, working over their faces with puffs and pencils, sleeking their hair, adjusting their hats with fractional precision above their eyebrows, turning their heads like birds with, sideways glances at their reflections… from behind the row of flush doors, at the back of the room, came intermittently the sound of cisterns emptying and refilling as the occupants pushed their way in and out. The persistent noise of the rushing water eventually caught Paula's attention, rousing her from her stupor of fatigue. She stood up and walked into a vacant lavatory.

She propped her handbag against the partition, which stopped a few inches above the floor; removed her shoes, and stepped up in her stockinged feet on to the seat. Very carefully, she lifted off the lid of the cistern and set it down against the pipes on the back wall. Then she took the little leather case from the shopping-bag and gingerly slid it down inside the cistern into the water. There was just room for it between the metal arm and the ball-cock. She pulled the chain and waited for the water to drain away and then gradually fill up once more till the ball-cock was in position. It was all right, the box was securely lodged without hampering the mechanism. And so long as it worked correctly, no one would need to examine it. She replaced the lid and climbed down. Her handbag had fallen on its side; she picked it up, put on her shoes, and walked out, a free woman at last…

8

"Right," said the man with the earphones, scribbling on a pad. He tore off the sheet and handed it across to his colleague at the desk behind him. "Report has just come through from the Swiss Customs: the Englishman in the Volkswagen GDX 2778 crossed into France at Chatelard yesterday just after 2 pm."

"Ah well, that takes it out of our manor," said the other, rubbing his hand over a yawn. "If anything's happened to him it's for the French police to deal with now. Better inform the St Gotthard, I suppose. If they want to make further inquiries it's up to them. But they won't," he added, rocking dangerously back on his stool to glance at the listless clock (another half hour before he came off duty). "Unless there's a wife, or some other interested party, to prod them." A look of intense absorption glazed his features. He vented an eructation. "I don't know why dumpling soup always gives me indigestion," he mused.

*

When Rex discovered he had lost track of her he was distraught. He ran frantically from street to street, hoping against dwindling hope that round the very next corner he might find her. He *had* to find her, it was imperative. He was sustained by the queer irrational belief that she would not make another attempt – at least so soon – to leave Paris. He had scared her off that one, he felt convinced. He knew the way her mind worked. She would have a superstitious fear of trying the same trick twice. And if he was right and she was still in Paris, he would find her. Somehow he would find her, he did not know how. "The situation," he quoted to cheer himself up, "is serious but not hopeless."

At one point, he found himself back in the Faubourg St Honoré where he had abandoned the Jaguar. It was gone of course. Presumably the police had removed it. Cars left unattended in Paris not only rendered their owners liable to a fine, but the cars themselves were impounded. Well, there was no time to attend to that now. It was safe enough where it was and he could collect it later.

He hesitated and glanced upwards, thinking: Oh, God, what am I to do? Where am I to look for her? Where shall I *go*?"; at which precise moment his upward glance was arrested by an enormous eye dangling half way up a building – a blank sky-blue stare framed in gold. An eye! It was like a holy vision telling him what to do.

Within five minutes, he was hunting through a *Trade and Professional Directory*. He noted down an address in the XIth *arrondissement*, and stepping into the street snapped up a taxi. He had twenty minutes in which to get there.

*

Paula felt curiously hollow and insubstantial, a sensation that was not physical but mental, as if she was not sure of her identity. It is an odd experience to have cut all ties, to find oneself suddenly alone. Utterly alone, and owning nothing but the clothes she stood up in and the money in her purse (a little more than enough to see her back to England – if that was what she wanted, but indeed what else was there for her to do?) To be strictly honest that was not quite all. There was also the money in their joint account in the Bank of Switzerland. There was nothing to prevent her drawing on that up to a thousand pounds, if she chose. And always providing Rex didn't draw it first. That of course would be the sensible thing for her to do. How could she expect to arrive in England without a penny, without a home, with nowhere to go? If she drew, say, two hundred and fifty pounds, that would see her through till she found a job. But she didn't want to touch his money, and the conflict made her tired, so tired suddenly she could hardly move one leg in front of the other.

She entered a café she was on the point of passing, and ordered a glass of coffee. "I could take a night-plane back, I suppose," she thought languidly, sipping the uninspiring mixture. "If that's what I'm going to do, I ought to start for the Airport right away." She opened her handbag to pay for the coffee... and – her heart seemed to heave over in her breast.

"Don't be silly, it can't be lost, you haven't looked properly," she admonished herself sharply. "Take out everything separately instead of scrabbling about like a frantic rabbit... it must be there... you're always imagining you've lost things."

But, "It isn't here... it's gone, it's gone!" her frightened mind declared, as she spilled the contents of her bag on to the table.

And indeed it was so. Her wallet, with all her money and travelers' cheques in it, was gone. All she possessed was a small coin-purse with a few francs of loose change in it. She was shaking from head to foot with the shock.

"I must have left it at the Printemps when I paid for the coat," she thought. "It's all right, they'll have it. I must go back there at once, before they close." She glanced at her watch and beckoned to the waiter. "What time do the big stores close?" she asked.

"Ah," he said, eyeing the clock above the *comptoir*, an air of polite regret in his tone, "they will have closed already, madame."

"Then I'm sunk," she thought. "Now I can't get away. I'm stranded. What am I to do?" Feeling sick with panic, she leaned her head on her hand, trying to collect herself. "I'll have to find somewhere to stay overnight, and then tomorrow, as soon as they open..." But they wouldn't be open tomorrow. *Tomorrow was Sunday.*

She shivered, drawing the black coat around her as if she were cold, and cast a helpless look around. The waiter approached again.

"Madame would like something else?"

"I wonder if you know of a hotel you could recommend, somewhere quiet and clean, and – cheap," she added faintly.

"But certainly, madame. My wife's cousin..."

As she walked slowly away with the address, she tried to recall exactly what had occurred when she paid for the coat. What made it so bewildering was that she remembered putting the wallet back in her bag. She clearly recollected putting it in her bag together with the bill. So she must have lost it after that.

After buying the coat, she had gone straight up to the Rest Room. She remembered placing the bag on the floor beside the partition in the lavatory, before she reached to lift off the cistern lid... she saw herself picking it up again: saw, as in a camera obscura, a small but distinct image of it lying on its side as she stooped to pick it up. And that was strange, for there was no reason why the bag should have fallen over, it had a flat base. It was disagreeably evident to her now what must have happened while she was occupied in concealing the leather box with its priceless contents. Someone in the adjoining compartment had slipped her hand through the gap between floor and partition, and deftly rifled the bag so conveniently placed there.

That was that then. No use in going back to the Printemps for it. It had been stolen. She was indeed stranded. Stranded in Paris without a penny to her name.

She stood on the kerb, clasping her hands so tightly in her distress that the square ruby pressed painfully into her finger. "My ring!" she thought. "I've got that. And my diamond wristwatch. Tomorrow – not tomorrow, but Monday – I can go to the Mont-de-Piété and pawn one or the other. Thank God, thank God," she murmured in relief: it was like being hauled out of a vast engulfing wave.

She became aware that a man was watching her, and she stepped hastily into the traffic tearing along the Avenue de la Grande Armée.

The man followed...

*

Rex went up two flights of dusty wooden stairs and rapped on the glass-paneled door at the top. The surroundings were hardly impressive. He tapped again. Through the frosted glass a rectangle of yellow light showed faintly from an open inner door. He turned the handle and walked in. Noted the shabby office, and marched across to the inner room.

Through the open doorway he saw, seated at a desk, a pale bluish-green wall behind him, a plump dark man negligently holding a telephone to his ear. By not so much as a flicker of his black enigmatic eyes did the man's face change its bland expression. He neither acknowledged the presence of his visitor – nor ignored it, for the sloe-shaped eyes traveled expressionlessly over the intruder's person, taking in his large frame, his bold blond physiognomy, and the style of his well-cut clothes, while he continued to lean the instrument against his ear without speaking. It seemed to be a remarkably one-sided conversation, for the man at the desk had not yet uttered a word. He picked up a pencil and made some marks on a piece of paper. "*Bien,*" he said at last and put the telephone back on its cradle. He stood up and held out his hand.

"Monsieur."

"Monsieur Hoquet?"

"Yes."

"My name is Vanbrugh."

"Enchanted to make your acquaintance, monsieur," said Monsieur Hoquet, looking supremely disenchanted. "You have not come on business, I hope. We are closed – officially, as you can see," he said, gesturing towards the empty outer office. "Perhaps you would call back after the holiday."

"This is a matter of extreme urgency. It can't wait. Presumably you have a special scale of charges to meet special requirements."

"*Ah, ça!*" murmured Monsieur Hoquet, with a slight movement of his hands. "In our unfortunate profession we are always under the obligation to assist clients when the matter is serious. Like doctors," he added, and the corners of his full mouth twitched. "Though in our case the obligation is less moral than financial."

"I am quite prepared to meet your terms."

"That will come later. First, I should like to hear what it is you require of us. Pray be seated, monsieur."

Rex favored him with a long steady glance.

"I want you to find my wife."

"Where?"

"Here in Paris."

"When did you see her last?"

"This afternoon." He lit a cigarette and blew out a feather of smoke. "I lost her in the Magasin du Printemps. We were shopping, and she went upstairs to buy some feminine article and... I never saw her again."

His dark eyes never wavering from Rex's face, Monsieur Hoquet said:

"Madame will have returned to the hotel by now, no doubt."

"Unfortunately, as it happens, we are not staying in Paris. We intended to continue our journey this evening."

"Ah? By car, evidently."

"Why do you say that?"

"Because, dear sir, if you were travelling by train or plane there would hardly be a problem; madame would await you at whatever terminal you were making your departure from. I therefore assume that though you gave madame time to return to the car when she did not come back you became anxious."

"Quite right."

"I ask myself one thing," Monsieur Hoquet said softly, measuring a paper-knife between his fingers. "Why you have come to me."

"I thought I had made that clear. I want you to find her."

"Why not the police, monsieur? They are the people for an affair of this nature. The police have every facility for locating missing persons. It is for them a simple matter."

"I prefer it to be handled privately. My wife would not like— It requires discretion."

"It is true the police are excessively inquisitive," agreed Monsieur Hoquet with a shadowy smile. "But so am I, monsieur. I cannot work without the facts."

"I have given them to you. What else do you want to know?"

"You have given me a version of the facts, I suggest. Let us be exact, I beg. Above all, exactitude, or we accomplish nothing!"

"I have told you all you need to know, I assure you."

"Except the truth. You see, I ask myself why if Monsieur Vanbrugh has an automobile he should arrive here by taxi? Ah yes, I heard the flag go up and then it drove away: one must have sharp ears in our profession and attentive minds. And then again, I think, it is so natural for a foreigner to go to the police when he is in difficulties, that it must be something quite special indeed to make him seek out a private investigator. And I am so curious I wonder why."

"Look here, Monsieur Hoquet—"

"You will tell me that these trivialities are not my concern. I know. But patience, my friend. Let us assume a hypothetical case: a man asks me to find his missing wife, but he does not tell me she has run away from him; it would be a sad waste of effort to look for a woman alone if she has in fact gone off with another man. You understand?"

"Very well," Rex said, crushing his cigarette. "She has run away. But not with anyone else. It's more simple than that, and more serious. We quarreled, and she suddenly jumped out of the car in the middle of a traffic hold-up. I had no idea where she was going. I didn't know how I should find her again if I let her out of my sight. I left the car there and went after her. I saw her enter the Magasin du Printemps, as I told you. She must have gone out by another door, for I scoured the building from top to bottom and found no trace of her. When eventually I got back to the car, that had gone too. I presume the police took it away, but I haven't had time to see to it yet."

"Your luggage was in the car?"

"Yes. But I am really not concerned about that, Monsieur Hoquet," he said, in irritation.

"Your wife left all her luggage behind when she jumped out of the car? She is of a very impulsive nature."

"She was very—" he hesitated over a choice of words "—upset," he concluded.

"She had much money with her?"

"Twenty or thirty pounds perhaps and some travelers' cheques."

"And her passport?"

"Yes."

"Well, that's better. You will give me the particulars and a description of your wife." And when he had noted these down, he said briskly: "*Bien, monsieur.* That will do for the present. I shall hope to have news for you in a few days."

"That won't do. I have to be in South America by Monday. You must find her at once. I can give you twenty-four hours, not any longer."

"My dear sir," said Monsieur Hoquet, almost laughing, "I am a private investigator, not a saint with miracles to command. It is Saturday evening and the office is closed for the holiday, as I explained when you came in. My employees will not be back until Tuesday morning."

"Offer them double time. Or hire other assistants. I have told you I don't care what it costs. I want her found, that's all that matters to me."

"If you are serious, monsieur, then you would be well-advised, as I suggested before, to go to the police. It is nothing of an affair to them to keep a check on all ports and terminals. Moreover, they have the registration of every foreign visitor in a hotel. Apply to them, monsieur."

Rex took out his wallet and laid fifty pounds on the desk between them. It was not necessary for him to say a word. Money speaks a language more potent than any human tongue. It exercises a peculiar fascination of its own, exciting cupidity even in the most wary.

Monsieur Hoquet did not touch it, did not look at it – after that first glance. His black enigmatic eyes stared unblinkingly at the man facing him.

Rex said:

"It is just as easy for you if you put your mind to it. You have only to telephone the hotels and ask if they have an Englishwoman called Mrs Vanbrugh staying with them. That's really all there is to it."

"What an imbecile," thought Monsieur Hoquet. Aloud he said: "My poor friend, have you any idea how many hundreds of hotels there are in Paris? It would require an army to make contact with them all."

"Then get an army," said Rex coolly.

For the first time, Monsieur Hoquet permitted a shade of emotion to appear on his round imperturbable face: he looked actually taken aback.

"You are not serious!"

"I could not be more so. This is a matter of life or death to me."

"Very well," agreed the other at last, rapidly reorganizing his ideas, his quick brain already working out a plan of campaign: ten men would be sufficient to cover the twenty districts of the city, each taking two districts and making his inquiries by telephone from his own home with the aid of a street directory; the task could be accomplished in a few hours. "Very well," he repeated, "it shall be done. But you realize that we may not be successful. It is possible, unless monsieur has some private knowledge he has not confided to me, that your lady will not go to an hotel."

"She must go somewhere, she can't spend the night on the street."

"It might be her instinct to get as far away from Paris as she can. It is a question of psychology."

"Precisely," Rex observed dryly. "It is a question of psychology."

"I have a contact at the Airport, I shall drop a word in his ear. And with your permission, monsieur, I will post an agent at the main stations – say, the Gares du Nord and de Lyons. We shall have no authority to detain her, of course. Would you wish our man to follow her, if he should spot her?"

"No. Just let me know where she's heading. As soon as there is any news, get in touch with me at the Hotel Royal. I shall expect to hear within twenty-four hours. Good night, monsieur."

"Well, well," mused Monsieur Hoquet, thoughtfully tossing a bunch of keys in the air as he watched from the window his visitor depart, "what a curious business. One wonders what is behind this quarrel. It must have been truly formidable for the woman to have leapt without warning from the car to run away from her husband. She runs, but not to another man. And she goes without luggage. And the husband does not go to the police. Because he is afraid of something. But what is it he is frightened of? It would be interesting to know.' Monsieur held one of the notes up to the lamp, and then swept it with the others into a drawer, which he locked. He sat down and reached for his file of addresses. He picked up the telephone.

"Guillaume? ...It is I, Lucien. Listen, are you at home this evening? I have a little job for you..."

*

AN EXTRACT from the evening edition of the *Eclaireur de Haute Savoie*:

A Disquieting Catastrophe.

A tragic and mysterious discovery was made last night in the Val d'Eon, below St Gervais-les-Bains, scene of several atrocious automobile disasters. The wreckage of a dark-green Volkswagen which had precipitated from the heights into the gorge beneath, completely destroying itself in the descent, was come upon by a farm laborer on his way home. One feared a fatality but, despite the most extensive examination of the territory, no trace of the unfortunate driver has come to light. At the same time, we learn that the automobile's owner, a M. Stefan Maddeux, of Great Britain, is reported to have disappeared. It is a mystery to baffle the police.

*

The large, well-dressed Englishman sauntered into the Hotel Royal, and asked for a single room.

"Yes, sir. For how long?"

"I am not quite sure. It depends how soon my business is completed. A week perhaps."

"We have a vacancy on the second floor. Would you like to see it? Georges, take the gentleman up to number 48. Is your baggage in the car, sir?"

The Englishman gave a dry laugh.

"Yes, unfortunately it is. And my car has just been stolen. Not a very happy start to a visit. I hope your police will be able to trace it without too much delay; though whether I shall be lucky enough to regain my luggage is open to doubt."

"How very regrettable," murmured the clerk, wondering whether to believe it, and decided to have a word with the manager while Georges escorted the Englishman upstairs. You don't have to be long in the hotel trade before you learn to recognize all the crooked gambits of tricksters.

On the other hand, it would be unfair to say such misfortunes never happened in life. The Englishman's story might be true, how could one tell? It was a dilemma best left to the manager's judgment.

It had been Rex's intention, on leaving Monsieur Hoquet, to go to the police and collect his car. He was more than a little disconcerted to realize suddenly, while he was still on his way there, that in making that reckless gesture of slapping down fifty pounds before Monsieur Hoquet he had left himself practically penniless. Now he would be unable to pay the police fine. He would have to leave it until Monday. A damned nuisance, but there was nothing else for it. As soon as the banks opened on Monday, he would cash a cheque. Meanwhile, he was not only short of money but he would have to present himself at the hotel without luggage, which, as well as being a personal inconvenience to himself, was something hotel managements understandably regarded with disfavor. He cursed his thoughtless act. It was not as though it had even been really necessary: Hoquet could have been persuaded without that. Damn Paula! this was all her fault. However, it should hardly be beyond his powers to invent some plausible tale to account for these tiresome circumstances (hence the story of the stolen Jaguar).

The hours passed with intolerable funeral pace, each dragging minute telling Rex that Hoquet had failed. He was half mad with anxiety by the time the phone rang the following morning, shortly after noon.

"The Hotel Obligado in the XVIIth *arrondissement*, behind the Avenue des Ternes," the speaker informed him.

"You are sure?"

"But certainly."

"There is one thing more. It is possible that the person in question might decide to leave before I am able to get there. I want the hotel kept under observation until, let us say, eight o'clock this evening."

"Understood."

*

The hotel was a narrow-fronted building in a quiet back street. From eight pm to nine-thirty, Rex waited in a café on the other side of the road, from where he could keep an eye on the hotel entrance. It had an oddly sinister air, as if it expected to be photographed for the public prints as the scene of some deplorable crime.

The summer night was falling and the dimly-lit sign opposite became visible against its darkening façade. Feeble illuminations gleamed through the doorway.

A porter in a mauve-striped jacket looked up from his newspaper.

"Monsieur?"

"I want to see Madame Vanbrugh. What is the number of her room?"

"I will inquire if it is convenient," said the porter, picking up the house phone.

"Don't bother: she's expecting me." Rex favored him with a friendly intimate smile. "I'm her husband," he said, drawing out his passport, and holding it open under the man's nose.

"Ah, in that case… if monsieur wishes to make her a little surprise, it is on the first floor, number 12. Would monsieur wish me to escort him?"

"I shall find it, my friend, don't trouble yourself." With his foot on the stair, he paused, and turned back. "Would there be a room vacant nearby for myself?"

The porter consulted the books.

"There is number 7. It is almost opposite madame's." He took down the key. "I will show monsieur."

Rex scribbled down the necessary details on the Questionnaire de Séjour and said in an undertone as they mounted the stairs: "After I have had a little word with madame, I will fetch the baggages from the station. I have only just arrived, you see."

"*Voici, monsieur*," said the porter, flinging open the door.

Rex laid a finger on his lips, nodding approval as he glanced inside. He slipped the porter a note, tiptoed across to number 12 and stood a moment in a listening attitude till the porter had turned the corner, and then went back to number 7, leaving the door ajar.

He sat on the edge of the bed, smoking one cigarette after another while he waited.

Once a man passed down the corridor humming and entered a door further along. A man and woman came by quarreling. Somewhere a woman laughed, a long silvery carillon. Through the wall the murmured talk changed to groans and love-cries.

At a quarter to eleven, he heard a door open and close, then light steps passing and the russle of silk. He peered through the crack and saw a woman in some sort of loose black wrap disappear at the end of the passage into a door marked *Salle de bain*. He recognized her by her hair and the poise of her head.

He gave her time to be safely immersed in the bath, and then he crossed the passage...

Her handbag was on the dressing-table; the empty shopping-bag lay on a chair, he was hardly surprised that the jewel case was not in it. He pulled open drawers one after the other: there was nothing in them but soiled lining-paper coated with a dusting of orange powder. The wardrobe exuded a smell of stale scent. The pale-gray silk hung in it like a ghost. He groped into the corners: someone had abandoned there, God knows how long ago, a repulsively dirty pink cotton-brocade girdle minus a suspender: Rex dropped it hurriedly.

There were so few places to look. He felt inside the bed and under the pillow. In the bed-table drawer was a shred of paper penciled with a phone number, and a french letter disguised as a metro ticket. He wondered wryly whether this was a courteous little attention on the part of the management for the convenience of their guests.

He passed his hand over the filth on top of the wardrobe: the case was not there. Nor was it under the chest of drawers. Nor on the ledge outside the window. It was not anywhere; therefore, he deduced, Paula must have taken it with her to the bathroom.

*

For Paula – staying in her room, feigning indisposition because she was afraid to venture out, and with nothing to eat since the morning *café complet*, because she had no money and this was the sort of hotel that did no catering beyond breakfast – it had been an interminably long day. There was nothing to do, nothing to read, nothing to help her pass the time but her memory. By way of distracting her thoughts, she recited all she could remember of Shakespeare, from Lady Macbeth to Desdemona, but these agonies of imaginary people served only to make her weep. Sometimes, her tears were for Stephen, sometimes they were for herself.

"It's hunger, my girl, that's making you feel so low," she admonished herself, blowing her nose. "Tomorrow everything will seem different. Once you get away from this horrible place, nothing will be so bad. As soon as you've got the money for the ring and can go..."

But it was precisely that which she could not decide – *where* to go. There seemed to be no other destination in all the world but this sordid room. It was as though she found herself relegated to some sad limbo from which there was no escape. She could not visualize a future. Her mind refused to take her beyond the desolating present. Life was meaningless without Rex, and impossible with him. She was imprisoned in a situation with no exit.

*

Rex was there facing her when she returned to the room.

"Hullo," he said.

"Hullo," she replied, her face taking on a greenish pallor beneath the sallow ochre light. She clutched together at the neck the black duster-coat she was using as a wrapper over her nakedness.

He smiled at her with antagonism.

"You've led me quite a dance."

"What do you want?"

"To see you, my dear. What else? You ran away so suddenly there was no time to discuss anything."

"I've nothing to discuss with you."

"My dear, don't be simple. You've managed to make a fine havoc of everything, haven't you? It's got to be put straight, in all fairness. I think we must really have a quiet little talk. Undisturbed," he added, turning the key in the door and dropping it into his pocket. He saw her eyes sidle to the phone an arm's length away. "I wouldn't," he said. "We don't want a scandal, do we?"

"I'm not coming back to you, Rex."

"I haven't asked you to," he remarked dryly.

"Then why are you here?"

"I think you know the answer to that one."

"Please say what you have to say, and go: I'm very tired." Indeed, she was suddenly aware of a dreadful fatigue. Her legs felt as though they could no longer support her. She sank down on the bed.

"All right," he said. "All right. I'm not going to beg you to come back, don't worry. If you want to leave me, go on. But there's a bit more to breaking it up than just walking out, you know. There's all the future to be settled. I want to be fair: I suggest we split our resources fifty-fifty."

"What resources?"

"The jewelery, primarily."

"I see. And you propose to give me half. That's generous of you."

"You're entitled to an equal share."

"I suppose I am – as your accomplice. I've shared equally in everything else, haven't I, all the unpleasantness and danger. But as it so happens, I wouldn't touch any of it."

"Then why, may I ask, did you run off with it clutched in your hand?" he queried with a sardonic twist of an eyebrow.

"It was a mistake. Call it a force of habit."

"It hardly seemed so to me, but let it pass. Have you considered how you're going to live, with no money to speak of?"

"That's my concern."

"Aren't you being rather stupid?"

"It's a matter of principle; I wouldn't expect you to understand."

"Oh, quite. Rather a new departure for you, too, isn't it?"

"Yes," she agreed simply.

He regarded her with a nonplussed frown.

"Well," he said at last, "if you've made up your mind it's not for me to persuade you. So, as I'm sure you're longing for me to be gone, if you'll just hand it over, I'll remove my odious presence."

"The jewelery? I can't. I haven't got it."

"No?" he said, quite mildly, watching her. "Where is it?"

"I don't know," she said, gripping the fingers of one hand tightly in the other. "I lost it."

Rex uttered a sound of laughter.

"Oh, come! You surely don't expect me to swallow that. What have you done with it?"

"I've told you: I lost it."

"You're lying."

"Why should I be lying? Didn't I just say I didn't want any of it?"

"You did. You did indeed. And I'm such a pathetic gull that I actually believed you. 'A matter of principle: you couldn't be expected to understand'," he quoted. "That's very winsome. If you want more than a half share, say so; but it's a little too much to expect me to surrender our entire fortune to you."

"Oh God," she said, weeping, "do let me alone! If you don't want to believe me, I can't help it. I haven't got the damned case. Look for yourself."

"I have. I'm perfectly aware it's not here, which is why I want to know where you've hidden it."

"Not anywhere where you can ever find it, you may be sure of that," she burst out. But directly the words were uttered, she recognized her blunder from the frightening manner in which he lowered his head like an animal about to charge.

"Really?" he said in a dead level tone.

She said quickly:

"If you want to know, it was stolen from me."

"Indeed? How did that happen?"

"Well..." She ran her tongue across her lips, "it was in a public lavatory. I put it down for a moment, and when I looked round it had gone – just like that."

"Go on."

"There's nothing more to tell."

"Isn't there? What did you do?"

She made a helpless gesture.

"Nothing. There wasn't anything I could do. I didn't see who'd taken it."

"Somebody walked off with over a hundred thousand pounds of jewelery under your very nose and you didn't do anything about it. My dear girl!"

"Well, what could I do? Be realistic. What good would it have done to scream out that I'd been robbed? You'd hardly want the police brought into it."

"Why not?"

In a low voice, not looking at him, she said:

"You know why not."

"I've run a great many risks for that money and a few more risks wouldn't frighten me off, you ought to know that. Or perhaps you never gave a thought to the insurance."

"The insurance?" Paula put her fingers to her mouth.

"Yes, my dear. If it's really lost or been stolen we have only to claim the insurance. Of course the loss must be reported to the police, that's obligatory in order to make a claim. Perhaps you didn't realize that?"

She stared at him in silence, turning white.

"Rex, listen to me! You mustn't try to claim the insurance. It would be fatal."

"To whom?"

"To you."

He broke into a laugh.

"Somehow I rather expected you to say that."

"To us both, then. To us both. Rex, you must believe me."

"You're like glass, Paula, you're so transparent I can see clean through you. But you're making the biggest mistake of your life if you are relying on the fond hope that I'll leave you a free hand to dispose of the jewelery to your sole advantage. Keep the jewelery if you must, it won't do you any good. The Policy is in my name. And whether the jewelery is lost or my wife made off with it when she left me, won't in any way affect the validity of my claim. You'll be picked up the first time you try to sell a piece."

"You fool," Paula said wearily, "you stupid fool! Do you think I'd be in a dump like this if I had the means to stay elsewhere? Disabuse yourself of the idea that I'm trying to take the jewelery from you in order to keep it for myself. Why, I might as well walk into the nearest police station and give myself up as an accessory to murder." She got up and moved across to the window, staring out into the gold-specked darkness. "All right. I was lying. The jewelery wasn't stolen."

"I knew that."

"I got rid of it. I had to. I didn't dare keep anything so dangerous to us both." Her fingers drummed nervously on the pane. "You see, there's something you don't know. Stephen had my emerald earrings in his possession when you shot him. He died with them in his hand." She turned and faced him. "*Now* do you understand why you can't claim the insurance? If you do, it's tantamount to asking to be charged with his murder – and they'll get me as accessory after the act."

He said slowly:

"No, I don't understand. I don't understand why he should have had the earrings."

"That's not important. He found them after we left. He was going to return them to me... when you killed him."

"Just a minute; not so fast. *Where* did he find the earrings?"

Paula hesitated for a fraction of a second.

"In his room. I was wearing them the evening you sent me to search it for evidence. But that's not the point. What matters is that once they're found on him, they provide evidence strong enough to get the pair of us hanged. Surely you can see that. You'll be walking right into their arms if you attempt to touch that jewelery or try to claim from the company. That's what I want you to grasp. That's all you need to understand."

"Is it? I don't agree. There's a great deal more to explain. If it's true, why did you keep it from me all this time, and why are you telling me now?"

She leaned her head on her hand.

"Oh, do what you like, only leave me alone! I no longer care what you do any more, I've come to the end. You did what was unpardonable: you killed a man without warning, and he was innocent. I told you he was innocent and you wouldn't listen. It was simply to give me back the earrings that he was following us that day. He knew they were valuable, and he didn't know where we were going or where we lived; he had no other way of getting them back to me."

"That's what he told you, and that's what you'd like to believe, no doubt. But it doesn't take account of the facts. It doesn't explain how he came to call me – I imagine, inadvertently – by my real name, or why he put through a long-distance call to London the previous evening."

Paula regarded him thoughtfully (thinking, 'What does it matter now'):

"He wasn't telephoning London; he was with me."

"What do you mean?" Rex said sharply.

"Just that. He was with me. Or I was with him, if you prefer."

"Why? Why did he pretend to me that he'd been telephoning? ..."

She arched her brows disdainfully.

"I asked him to, if you must know. What happened was, he came in unexpectedly and caught me searching his room."

"You never told me," he said suspiciously.

"No. I never told you. But that was when I knew for certain that we had nothing to fear from him. He hadn't been sent to run us to earth, or he would have at once realized why I was there. There could be only two reasons why I should be in his room uninvited. I said nothing, I waited to see what his reaction would be. And he assumed I'd come there to be alone with him for a few minutes, poor darling..." She gave a small wincing laugh and turned her face aside

174

"And you let him believe it."

"Naturally I let him believe it."

"You let him make love to you." His nostrils made white accents either side of his nose.

"What else could I do?"

A great shiver ran over him.

"You just took off your clothes and went to bed with him, didn't you? ...That was where you left the earrings! Wasn't it? My God, you slut!" A terrible rage boiled up in him. "It's you who's brought this ruin upon us both! You filthy slut... you whore... you damned whore..." he stuttered, grinding the expletives between his clenched teeth as he shook her.

In a half-strangled voice, she tried feebly to utter:

"Don't..."

"Did you enjoy your coupling, you dirty bitch...? Did he pleasure you...?" He sobbed the words out breath-lesslv, in a blind fury of sexual jealousy. Images of torturing familiarity presented themselves to his mind.

Consciousness dwindled to a pinpoint, a spark that signaled to her brain: "He's killing me... he doesn't realize what he's doing..." She began to think, "Now he'll never escape—" but before she could reach the end of her thought, time had ceased.

Her soft pliant neck went slack in his grasp. He stared down at her incredulously.

"Paula!" he said. "Paula!"

Soundlessly his lips formed the words: "I didn't mean..." He drew his hands away and watched her crumple limply to the floor. His heartbeats hammered in his head as if some desperate prisoner inside was trying to get out. But his mind was numb, too numb even to understand what had happened. His brain had ceased to register.

"What have I done?" he kept thinking stupidly. "I didn't know what I was doing... she's dead. I've killed her. How could she have died so easily? I never meant to hurt her..."

Her lifeless body was terribly heavy in his arms as he gathered her up and laid her on the bed. Her open bloodshot eyes stared past him indifferently. With a delicate disbelieving gesture, his fingers touched the grape-dark bruises on her throat and slid down to her breast. He flung himself across the body with an agonized cry. He had lost her forever. And without her he was lost himself.

He became aware of a mechanical voice repeating monotonously over and over without looking for an answer: "What am I to do? …Dear God, what am I to do? …" and at length, the meaningless phrase roused an alarm in his brain. He sprang to his feet. He had to get away. He had to get away at once.

He clasped his cheeks, drenched in a wave of panic. *They would know he had killed her.* He had been seen entering the hotel, the porter would be able to describe him. The porter knew his name, he had said he was her husband and had shown him his passport. His name and description would be in every police station, at every port.

He had only until the body was discovered in which to escape. *A few hours, that was all.* It gave him one chance, one slender chance, if he left at once, to get out of the country, as far away as he could, immediately.

And *immediately* was impossible. He hadn't the *means*. Until the banks opened, he was penniless. And the banks would not be open until *ten o'clock.*

"Christ," he thought. "I daren't wait till then; it may be too late." But he knew he would have to wait. There was no other way.

He looked at his wristwatch: it was a little after two. An hour at which the night-porter might well be nodding in his pen; he wondered whether he'd be able to creep out unseen. He wondered whether there would be a different porter on duty now, who, if he saw him, would take him merely for one of the casual night trade.

Every nerve in his body urged him to escape, to get away while he could; a different fear caused him to linger: the frightful consideration that once he was gone he could no longer prevent the discovery. She might have left word to be called at eight… at seven… at six even, and he would never know how little time was left to him. There was only one way to make sure, and that was to stay here, in this dreadful room – with her, until he could go to the bank. The notion filled him with horror. He moved away from the bed on trembling legs. He tried to occupy his mind with plans. He had a great deal to think about if only he could think…

10

Slowly, gray light slanted through the window. He heard hooters blowing. A church nearby rang out a peal of bells. The muffled throb of traffic caused the window to shiver in its frame.

At nine o'clock, he locked the door and went downstairs. With an effort, he mustered a pleasant smile for the porter.

"A barber," he said, rubbing his knuckles against his bristly chops. "I'll be back shortly. Don't disturb madame while I'm gone, she wants to sleep." He could feel the sweat soaking into his collar as he walked away.

Skimpy little girls, strolling arm in arm, made roguish eyes at him, giggling, as he passed. He had the uncomfortable sensation that there was something ludicrous about him of which he was unaware. His sense of isolation was heightened by the air of unwonted gaiety that seemed to affect the atmosphere.

From the Place des Ternes, he caught an autobus to the Boulevard des Capucines, where his bank was situated. He noticed a number of shops that had not yet taken down their shutters.

When he reached the bank, it was still closed, though it was a quarter after ten. He crossed the road and entered a café. Standing at the counter, stirring his coffee, he said casually to the proprietor:

"Do you happen to know what time the banks open?"

"Today?"

"Yes." He was gripped by a sudden apprehension without knowing why.

"Ah, monsieur, but they do not open today. It is the Fourteenth of July."

"The Fourteenth of July?" he stammered.

"Our national holiday, monsieur: the celebration of the Fall of the Bastille."

*

177

His mind must have gone quite blank, for he had no recollection afterwards how far he had walked or how long he had been sitting on this bench under the plane trees.

"I am done for," he thought numbly. "I am done for. There's nothing I can do now. Nothing at all."

The Fates had outwitted him with superb simplicity. The divine irony underlying the nature of things had rendered his escape impossible by making this the very day in the year when all financial settlements came to a standstill. A million banks could open their doors tomorrow but it would be no use to him. Tomorrow was too late.

By tomorrow, everyone would be looking for Ross Vanbrugh. The money would lie in the bank forever and ever, untouched. It was a wry thought. For never had anyone needed money more. With money, he could get himself a forged passport. Without it, he had no means on earth of getting away.

All he owned was in the Jaguar and the Jaguar was in the custody of the police. Even if he contrived to raise the money to pay the police fine, the car was no good to him any longer, he could never make his get-away in that, for they knew the registration number and once they had seen his driving-licence and passport they had him in their hands; it would be the easiest thing in the world for them to pick him up. ("Wanted for Murder, Ross Vanbrugh, English, driving a cream Jaguar, number AGH 1324...")

So it came to this: he possessed nothing but the clothes he stood up in. No other means of any kind. Not so much as the price of a night's lodgings. He was going to starve, with thousands in the bank he dared not claim and a fortune somewhere in precious stones that he would never find. He thought:

"God, what am I going to do!"

He was a foreigner. Unmistakably. His French was fairly fluent, but he could never hope to pass for a Frenchman. He could not get any sort of a job, not even as a casual laborer, without a permit, and he had no *carte d'identité*. In fact, such means of identification as he had, he realized with a sinking heart, were supremely dangerous to him. He thought:

"I must destroy Ross Vanbrugh!"

He looked round to see whether he was being observed, but the passersby flowed by without a glance at him. He took out his passport and, leaning forward where he sat, dropped it through the grating in the gutter into the sewer below. It gave him a strange pang to see it go. Piece by piece he tore up his papers, letters, travelers' cheques, and watched the fragments flutter away into the darkness under the iron grid.

Now, he had no identity. Officially, he had ceased to exist. He was no one. A man without a name, without a nationality, without rights, without means of subsistence. There was nowhere for him to go, yet he could not stay where he was, he had to keep going. He was a man on the run, with nowhere to run to.

He got up from the bench and walked slowly away to seek a night's lodging in some narrow alley between two houses or under a bridge or in some deserted shed, among the other outcasts, the derelict, the scavengers of dustbins…

*

On October 3rd, a vagrant, caught breaking into a farmhouse some fifteen miles north of Arles, was taken into custody by the police. He had on him no means of identification and refused to give his name. The unknown man was detained pending inquiries.

Printed in Great Britain
by Amazon